**"HEY HE'S GETTING AWAY!"
CAME A YELL FROM OUT FRONT.**

"He's got my best horse!" I made my way to the front street, heard the blacksmith cussing something fierce as whatever was left of the band of looters rode out of town.

"Not for long, he ain't," I said, calm and determined. "Which one is he?" I asked as I took aim with Mister Henry.

"Second from the right, the bay."

No sooner had he said the words than I squeezed the trigger and the man on the bay was a part of the dust being left behind by the riders. . . .

Fawcett Gold Medal Books
by Jim Miller:

CAMPAIGNING

COMANCHE TRAIL

GONE TO TEXAS

ORPHANS PREFERRED

RIDING SHOTGUN

SUNSETS

WAR CLOUDS

MISTER HENRY

Jim Miller

FAWCETT GOLD MEDAL • NEW YORK

For Cindy and Doris, who know just what Charlie Russell meant when he said, "Any man who can make a living doing what he likes is lucky, and I'm that." They're two fine young ladies.

Chapter 1

Women have always raised the most hell in my life. But I reckon that's the way it is with most men. We get around some healthy-looking woman and all of a sudden we've got the worst case of cross-eye and tanglefoot of the tongue that you could ever imagine. I ought to know; that's how it was with me when I met my own wife so many years ago. But I figured waiting there at the stage depot for Callie, my younger sister, couldn't be all that dangerous. After all, how much trouble could a sister get you into?

She was the prettiest girl you ever did see, especially when you consider that us Hooker men tended toward ugliness. I hadn't seen her since she was fourteen, and even then those fancy things Ma gave her to wear . . . well, let's just say that above the waist and below the neck . . . she was growing, if you know what I mean. I was at least twenty years older than she was, but then, keeping track of my age was never a strong point with me.

What was going on in Independence, Missouri, that spring of 1863, on the other hand, was a lot uglier than Callie would ever get. They were calling it the War Between the States and a lot worse, but all I wanted was to be left alone by it. Surviving in this land fighting your own wars was hard enough without having to fight someone else's, I always figured.

"What do you think about the war?" the bartender said, drawing me another beer. I was sitting in a saloon not far from the depot. The barkeep wasn't too awful old, maybe thirty, but friendly enough for being as sawed-off as he was.

"I'm trying not to think about it." There's been some who say I sound surly when I talk, and maybe that's so, but I'll guarantee you'd be acting the same way if it was pushing midday and the ten o'clock stage hadn't rolled in yet!

"How long you been here?" was his next question. They also say I sometimes ain't too sociable, which could be true.

"Ever since you decided to open up and let me in this morning, son. Now, why don't you give me another dose of whatever it is I'm drinking and let me do just that."

"I meant how long have you been in town?"

"Son, you just don't give up, do you?" I gave him a hard look as he set down the beer.

"All right, mister, don't get edgy." He wandered off to take care of another handful of customers, the saloon having gained a few more patrons in the last half hour. When he made it back to my end of the bar, I tried being a bit easier on the man.

"Look, son, I got a sister coming in on a stage that's overdue. Then I got to escort her to an aunt who's uglier than some Injuns I've seen!" I must have sounded like a desperate man the way I was talking.

"In that case, I can understand how you feel," the barkeep said. "Got one of them old maid aunts myself." He shook his head in despair. "Cusses worse than I do. Can you believe it?"

I nodded. "Same with mine."

He smiled before moving on. "Next one's on me."

Someone gave out a yell outside and I heard the six-horse hitch pound past us down the street. There are sounds you get used to in this country, and the stage rolling into town was one of them. I grabbed up my rifle and headed for the depot, not half a block away.

It wasn't hard recognizing Callie, for she was the only woman on the coach and sure enough was drawing a crowd.

Not that that was unusual; a new woman arriving in town tended to do that in any of these half-civilized towns west of the Mississippi, and some on the east side, too.

"Bodacious beautiful, like I heard a fella say one time," I said, making my way through the crowd as she looked around trying to find a familiar face. But it was my voice she recognized first, her face coming to a full flush, then she looked my way and smiled.

"Ezra!" she yelled out, throwing her arms around me and giving me what I reckon she figured was a bear hug. Oh, I winced all right, but it wasn't from that hug she was giving me. When she let go, she glanced up at me with that easy smile I remembered. "You never could stand that name, could you?"

"Hell, no!" I replied. "Do you know how many fights I've gotten into over it?" Then we both laughed as the crowd thinned out and each of us took to studying how much the other had changed over the course of a decade.

"Pardon me, sir, but I don't think you should be using such vulgar language around this lady." The man saying it was maybe ten years older than Callie and as fancified an easterner as you could imagine, bowler hat and all.

"I wouldn't push it, mister," I said over Callie's shoulder. "She's heard worse than the word 'hell' from me."

"But—"

"Oh, excuse me," Callie said, all of a sudden back in the present. "I'm terribly sorry. Ezra, this is Robert Carston. We've ridden most of the trip from Philadelphia together." She had a look about her when she said it, sort of like she was proud of the fact that she was presenting this yahoo to me. "Ezra is my brother."

I could tell he wasn't looking forward to this introduction any more than I was, as much starch as he had in his collar all of a sudden.

"It's nice to meet you, Ez—"

"You call me Black Jack, if you've got any sense," I said, cutting him off with another hard look. "Last man called me *Ezra* is still trying to straighten out his beak." Callie was right about me not liking the name, but I'd wait some to tell her how a card game had gotten me my new moniker. "I'd shake, but I got Mister Henry in one hand"—I held out my Henry repeater rifle—"and my sis in the other." I smiled at her, ignoring this Carston fellow.

"Other than the beard, I don't think you've changed at all," she said, returning the smile.

"That's what Pa always said. The women in the Hooker family have all the beauty. Us boys tend to have a bit of the oak tree in us." Callie blushed and I let go of her, picking up the trunk that had been deposited next to her by the driver. One thing about a good-looking woman, she can get damn near everyone to do for her without even having to ask.

Springtime usually brought the rains in those parts, but the past week had been fairly dry, so mister fancy pants didn't have to worry about getting his spiffy new coat muddied up escorting Callie to the boardwalk. Of course, I didn't see him look too anxious to reach down for that trunk.

"Got a room for you at the hotel down the other end of the block," I said, and began walking. "First I got a stop to make."

The saloon I'd been cooling my heels in that morning was on the way to the hotel, so I figured I'd take that barkeep up on his invite while he still had it in his memory. Some folks develop awful poor memories when it's convenient for them.

I set the trunk down in front of the saloon and was about to enter when I stopped. A frown crossed my face as I glanced down at the trunk, then at Carston. What the hell, Callie must have seen something in the poor sap.

"Want a beer?"

"Why . . . yes." He seemed genuinely surprised at the offer.

I picked up the trunk and pushed my way inside the batwing doors, setting it down just inside the door as Callie and the pilgrim entered and my eyes adjusted to the darkness. Everyone else's eyes seemed to be focused on Callie, not that you could blame them. If you found a woman in an establishment that was strictly for men, she was usually a barmaid or a whore. A decent woman wouldn't be caught dead in a place like this saloon, which only made me wonder how much hell I was going to catch from Aunt Sarah when she heard about the first place I'd taken her niece when she arrived in Independence.

The table next to the entrance was occupied by a couple of drifters, by the looks of them. Not that I hadn't looked just as scraggly as they did at one time or another, but they didn't seem like any too permanent a part of the population, so I figured that was the table I'd take.

"Lady needs a seat," I said. I tried to sound as polite as I ever did around Mama, but the look on my face told these two something different.

"What?" The one who spoke sounded about as incredulous as Callie's pilgrim had when I asked if he wanted a beer. Could have been something going around, I reckon, but more likely this was a case of flat-out dumbness. Some folks don't catch on too quick.

"I said the lady needs a seat." Mama never did care for the tone of voice I was using now, but since it was these two drifters and not Mama I was facing, I really didn't give a damn. And to make sure they knew it, I brought the barrel end of Mister Henry down hard right in the middle of the table. There was one each to the right and left of the rifle barrel, and it didn't make no never mind to me which one's nose I busted first. "Now, you can be gentlemanly about it or you can wind up bleeding, but I'm a-gonna have this table for the lady. Understand?"

They understood.

"All right," the frazzled one said, picking up his bottle. "Come on, Frank, we been sitting long enough, anyway."

When we all had a seat, Slim, or whatever the barkeep's name was, came over to take our order. I got that free beer he'd mentioned and one for Carston, but Callie only asked for a glass of water. Never was much of a drinker, she.

"Changed quite a bit since last time I seen you, Callie." I'm not one of those great orators like that Webster fellow, so short and blunt is about as stylish as I get when it comes to words. Trouble was, Callie was waiting to hear what I had to say about her changing; I could see that in the way she looked at me. "Beauteous best describes it," I said, feeling the blood run hot under my neck hairs.

"Beauteous?" Carston gave me an odd look as the barkeep set down the drinks.

"Well, that and . . . well, uh"—I swallowed hard and gulped down half the beer in one swig—"damn, Callie, but them shirts Mama give you sure have growed some!" Carston was getting flustered again, Callie had a pleased look about her, and I quickly swallowed the rest of that beer, hoping it would take my mind off these so-called pleasantries we were supposed to be exchanging.

"What in the world are you talking about?" For the first time since I'd met him, Carston was showing some gumption, putting some force behind his words. Maybe he did have some bottom after all.

I never did get a chance to explain, for trouble took over then, and I just knew that the whole day was shot to hell and gone.

"What he means is she's a real screamer," the fellow whose seat I'd taken said, approaching the table again and drunkenly glancing down at Callie. His partner wasn't too far behind him and looked just as ugly.

"See here, my good man," Carston said, only this time he didn't get to impress anyone at all, for a big steady hand fell onto his shoulder, keeping him in place as he began to rise.

"See here?" one of the drifters mimicked in a bad version of what you might call educated eastern talk.

"My good man?" The other one was just as bad.

I don't think it was that Robert Carston was scared so much as that he just couldn't move with that big hand planted on his shoulder. Who knows, maybe he'd have gotten up and done these two in, had things been different. Trouble is you can't go through life predicting what might have happened when you've got to deal with the here and now. And putting it off never makes it any better.

I stood up slow and stretched like I would have any other

time the ache in my bones got to bothering me. That sort of relieved Carston of having to impress these lads, for they had their eyes on me now. My Henry was leaning up against the wall, about three feet out of reach, and these fellows were armed with pistols anyway, which I reckon is what made them feel they had the floor to themselves. Maybe they did, maybe they didn't.

"Feeling right wolfish today, are you, boys?" I said it as conversationally as I could, although if one of them had looked close he'd have seen a whole lot of red crawling up the back of my neck—all because of what he'd said about my sister. Just as casually, I picked up my mug of beer and swallowed the last of the contents. The whole thing was getting Robert Carston mad, and that was good, for sooner or later he'd have to find out that tough talk ain't nothing more than hot air out here unless you can back it up.

"No more'n you were when you took our table," the drunk finally replied.

I smiled briefly. "Oh, that wasn't wolfish, boys; that was my natural style. Ask anyone."

"You're past your time, old man," he said, taking in the buckskins and beaver hat I wore. "Better go back to them mountains and leave us alone."

"Now, Robert," I said to Callie's newfound friend, "this here's a lesson to be learned about living in the west. First off, you see, drunks are just as loud-mouthed out here as they are back where you come from." That didn't set too well with these two yahoos, which was fine with me.

"Indeed," Carston said, real calm all of a sudden. He glanced over his shoulder, taking in just where it was the man with the hand on his shoulder was situated. Fact is, I got the feeling he might just know what I had in mind. "And what would you say is the second?"

"Second is you just don't never know how many weapons you have at your disposal."

Then I gave him a demonstration.

Now, hoss, I may be a bit past my prime, but that don't mean I ain't learned a lesson or two. I can be downright fast when the occasion calls for it, and the drunk standing next to Callie hardly knew what hit him when I brought that thick mug up alongside his skull. It knocked him off balance, but not out, so I hit him on the face a couple more times and once or twice on top of the head for good measure until he was laid out on the floor just a wee bit unconscious.

"Well, now, Robert," I said, turning to my rear, "I never did go in much for hide-out guns, but I'd say you done right well for yourself." And he had. Out of the corner of my eye, while I was swinging that beer mug, I'd seen him bring his elbow back alongside his chair into the other fellow's elsewheres. I don't know where he got that derringer he was holding now; but stuck up underneath that man's chin, it had his attention, it surely did.

"Purely obfuscating, ain't it?" I said to Callie, who looked just that. Confusing is what it means, case you ain't had a good dose of my ways yet.

"Is he going to live?" Callie glanced past me to the man I'd tangled with, apparently more interested in his health than in mine. That was another question I never got to answer, for all of a sudden she had a look of stark terror about her. Instinct is how you stay alive out here and I knew that look. I was half turned around, pulling the knife out from over my shoulder, when I heard Slim, the bartender, yell out "Don't," followed a split second later by a pistol shot. By the time I was facing him full, the man on the floor was dead, a half-cocked pistol in his hand.

"He was gonna back-shoot you," Slim said by way of explanation. "I don't allow shooting in this place."

"Obliged."

"Mister, you get the hell out of here and don't never come back," Slim said to the yahoo Carston still had the drop on. What that barkeep lacked in size he made up for in the size of the barrel of that Colt he was holding. "And take him with you."

I'll guarantee you the ruffian who was still alive was now stone-cold sober as he dragged his friend from the saloon. I also noted a look in his eye of what could only be described as vengeance as he glanced our way. Another one of my gut feelings is what I had then; he wanted me to know I hadn't seen the last of him.

"A bit chipped, but it's mostly on the bottom," I said, handing the battered mug to Slim at the bar. "If it don't leak too much, I'd appreciate another of these at the table, and one for my friend. Then we'll be on our way."

Slim nodded silently, giving me what I reckon you call your average bartender's smile, accommodating if not sincere. At the table, Carston was making sure Callie was all right. I said nothing until the barkeep brought the drinks and another glass of water for Callie.

"You didn't have to watch my back like that, you know. Could have gotten you into a peck of trouble."

Slim shrugged and smiled. "Wouldn't be nothing I ain't been in before. Besides," he added, tossing a shy glance at Callie, "I got a sister of my own, so I know how it is."

"So you don't go in for hide-out guns, eh?" Carston said with a grin. I reckon there's nothing like a good back-to-back fight to make you take notice of the other fellow's worth, even if you are a bit shy of him. Callie's friend was finding that out about me, and, truth be known, I reckon I was beginning to discover the same in him.

"Guns, no." I pulled out the tinker throwing blade I kept in a small sheath tied to a worn piece of buckskin string that hung about my neck. "Knives is something else again. That and long guns," I added, nodding toward Mister Henry still leaning up against the wall. Carston was blind if he hadn't already seen the big bowie knife at my side.

The conversation sort of dried up on my end about then as Callie and Robert, as she seemed fond of calling him, told me all about their trip from back east to Independence. Mind you, it wasn't as interesting as some of those stories I've heard in the mountains, but she was my sister, so I took it all in like one of those fellows who've been away from civilization so long they'll halt a wagonload of pilgrims for a day or so just to find out what's going on three territories back. By the time Robert had started to talk about this Emancipation Proclamation speech Lincoln had given after they fought some battle in a place called Antietam, I started to notice that the saloon had gotten real scarce of customers.

"Your story's gonna have to wait, Robert," I said, then nodded toward Slim, who had a couple of pistols sitting on the counter and was in the process of producing more from his small armory. I pushed my chair back and grabbed up the Henry.

"Getting to be time to provide today's meat for the fire, is it?"

Callie and Robert seemed a bit confused, but Slim knew what I was talking about.

"Ain't so much hunting as being hunted, friend," he said, laying yet another pistol on the bar. "Seems that fella I killed has got friends in town who are more concerned about revenge than learning right from wrong."

"What's going on?" Robert asked.

I ignored the question. The sound of a mob down the street heading our way was enough to tell me this wasn't a time for talking as much as for doing.

"Robert, you turn over a couple of these tables and get Callie behind 'em. Then grab yourself up whatever we don't take off'n the bar, and if it ain't me or Slim comes back in through those doors, *kill the bastards*!"

"I'm the one they're after, you know," Slim said as I tucked two cap-and-balls in at my waist.

"First thing Pappy taught us was you always pay your debts."

The smile on his face was one of pure appreciation.

They were halfway down the block; no less than fifty, no more than a hundred by my count. Loud and noisy, like all mobs. All of them had pistols, but it was rope justice they were interested in more than anything else. In a matter of seconds they were there before us in the street.

"You can't do that, Hardesty," said the ruffian who'd tangled with Robert Carston's derringer.

"Could be, but I did," Slim said, just as angry. "You know the rules in my place. No shooting. Besides, your

friend was getting ready to back-shoot this man.'' He nodded toward me.

"He's right, fellas. Best you wait for the law to show
up and we'll talk about it. Way I figure it, only one who's
gonna make a profit out of this fight is the undertaker,'' I
said.

A few in the rear chuckled, but for the most part they
all showed how angry they could look.

"No.'' The loudmouth was talking again. "I don't know
who the hell you think you are, old man, but I want him
and I'm taking him!'' He took a step forward and I levered
a round into my Henry and pointed the rifle right at him.

"I know who I am, sonny.'' Most of these men were
tending toward what you call middle age, but when you've
been around as long as I have . . . well, they ain't nothing
but pups by comparison, so I call them all "son.'' "Black
Jack Hooker's my name, and the pure fact is that I've got
a sprinkling of everything from lion down to skunk in me;
and afore this war you're fixing to start's over, you may
just figure me for one of them fancy zoological institutes
back east! Now, if you want Slim, you just go right ahead
and make your move, sonny.'' Then, looking out over the
crowd, I added, "I can oblige any of the rest of you who
feel the same way.''

I do believe I could have tanned and sewed up a decent
pair of moccasins and not heard any noise excepting that
of the needle; the tension was that thick. Then the silence
was broken by the appearance of two people I hadn't expected.

Robert Carston was the first, walking out of the saloon
with a sawed-off shotgun in hand. Anyone would guess he
was a pilgrim from his dress, and he gave a convincing
performance of it as he fumbled with the shotgun, acting
the totally ignorant tenderfoot.

"Isn't this what you westerners call a scatter-gun?'' he
asked no one in particular, although he had positioned himself next to Slim. Robert's voice had taken on the damnedest English accent. "We have guns like this in England,

you know, but with much longer barrels. Let's see, which one do you cock first?''

"Hold on there, mister," one of the crowd warned as he pulled back one of the triggers. "You could get somebody hurt doing that."

Robert was oblivious to the man's comments.

"Now, which trigger is the one for this barrel?" It was almost laughable, the way he was asking for assistance from a mob that was on its way to stampeding him.

"Don't listen to him!" the loudmouth yelled. "He's bluffing! I say rush 'em!"

They were just getting ready to when I heard the loud click of Robert's second hammer being pulled back. Then this tall, lanky fellow stepped up beside me. He had two Colts out, and one of them snapped off a shot that ricocheted near the loudmouth's feet.

"Maybe he's bluffing, but I'm not." He could have been twenty-five and stood a muscular six feet plus. There wasn't anything hard about his voice as he spoke, but you can bet the men in the front of the mob listened to him—if not to his voice, then to his guns.

"All right, Bill," one of the men said after a pause. Then, throwing me a look that said he'd get even, he added, "Come on, boys, let's go home. When the marshal gets back he can look into it."

It was as if this Bill character had some mystical power over them, the whole lot of them. One minute they were ready to rush us, going up against a shotgun, a handful of pistols and Mister Henry; a guaranteed dozen gunshot wounds at least. Then this fellow in a wide-brimmed flop hat shows up with two Colts and you'd think it was Ezekiel himself passing out hell! Not that I didn't appreciate it, mind you—it just didn't make any sense.

"You've got a lousy choice in friends, mister," the stranger called Bill said when the mob had dispersed.

"Oh, I don't know," I said. "Wouldn't you stand by a man who'd just saved your life?"

Bill raised his eyebrows. "Adds a bit to the story."

"Slim, why don't you put away that hardware of yours and go back to tending bar," I said. Then, looking at Bill, I added, "Seems I owe you at least a beer."

Chapter 2

He wouldn't say nothing more than that it was true his name was Bill, but that was more than some I'd met would give out, so I didn't pry any further in that area. Of course, about halfway through that beer I found out that it hadn't just been seeing three men bucking the odds that made him deal a hand in our game. No, sir. Old Bill here, he had problems of his own a-brewing.

"For a man as soft-spoken as you are, friend, you sure did give those fellas out there a mean look," I said. "Or was it just your guns they was interested in?"

Bill smiled, slowly glancing over toward Callie.

"If I'd known you were fighting over a lady as pretty as this one, I'd have jumped in sooner." Callie blushed, and Robert, well; he looked like he was just tolerating this stranger for the good deed he'd done. It was me Bill was talking to now. "Reckon I've had a streak of flat-out mean in me the past couple of days."

I raised a curious eyebrow. "That so." See, it ain't all that hard to get a man to talking about what ails him. But then, I reckon it never has been.

"I was bringing a partial load from Fort Leavenworth to Sedalia," he began in that soft voice of his.

"Freighting for the army, you say?" Trouble with these young pups is they figure us old bastards are addled, feeble, and anything else you want to throw into the pot, when the fact is we can do about twice as much as they can. But

14

we let them think what they like until the time's right; there ain't nothing like a winning hand to make a fellow sit up and take notice. No, sir.

"That's right. I was supposed to finish up loading in Springfield for General Curtis and his army. He's been working somewhere out of southwest Missouri and northwest Arkansas, you know."

"No, I didn't." Not that I really cared, either. Like I said, when it came to this war . . .

His face got grim now as he remembered what it was that had gotten him all riled in the first place.

"We weren't far into Jackson County when we got hit by a band of rebels. We gave them a fight, but there was just too many of them." He paused, and it was a cautious one; I'll say that. "They've got my wagons, supplies, and men. I think I'm the only one that got away."

I knew then why he'd paused. Robert Carston and Callie may not have understood, but I did. And you can bet I wasn't about to say anything right then to him about it. Hell, the man had saved my life not an hour ago!

My sister and her friend seemed too taken with the conversation we were holding to want to butt in like others might, and for that I was glad. At least I had a sister who knew she was in a man's world now.

"Well, now, friend, looks like you got yourself into a mite of a spot."

Bill's smile was sheepish. "A considerable spot," he admitted.

"How'd you come to Independence?" Mind you, it wasn't that I doubted the boy. You just get used to feeling your way around and finding out as much as you can before you get out your shopping list. If you've ever been to the general store and plunked down more goods on the counter than you had silver to pay for them, well, you know what I mean. Me, I was curious as to what kind of trouble I was getting into.

"Aside from the fact that Independence was nearby and the county seat, I thought I'd get some help and go get my wagons back." Bill wasn't in too friendly a mood, if I judged the reading of his face right. A defensive frown had replaced his easygoing manner, and I knew that if he were pushed any further he'd be right on the edge of exploding, and I didn't want that at all.

"Well, if that mob was any sample of the men in this town," Robert said, "I doubt you'll find much sympathy for your needs after what you did today."

Bill shrugged, knowing the pilgrim was right.

"Tell you what, Bill," I said, finishing my beer. "I got nothing to do for the next day or so. What say we take us a ride out to where you lost your rigs and see can we get 'em back?"

Bill was surprised, but it was Callie who spoke up.

"What about Aunt Sarah? Don't we have to be getting on to Lawrence?" Anyone else might think she was perturbed because I'd be putting myself in danger, but I knew she was really worried about angering Aunt Sarah, the terror of the Hooker family.

"Callie, when's the last time you saw Sarah?"

"Why, when I was a child, I suppose. It's been some time."

"What do you remember about her?"

"Well," she faltered, "I don't think she was very nice to me."

"Right," I said. "Look, Callie, that woman was hatched out of the egg full-growed and ugly and mean to boot, and she ain't going to get any nicer in the next couple of days." Both Callie and Robert were taken aback, but Bill was beginning to smile some when I turned to him. "Getting your wagons back is going to be tarnational easy compared to living anywhere close to Aunt Sarah, son, so you round up a handful of pistols and meet me wherever it is they serve up a decent meal before daybreak around this place. Don't want to burn too much daylight."

The lad was puzzled. "Just a handful of pistols and *you*?"

"Oh, I'll bring Mister Henry, of course." I smiled, nodding toward the wall my rifle leaned against, but it didn't do much good for an explanation. "Look, son, these soldier boys, Rebs, Yanks—I don't care which ones—they don't know nothing 'bout Injun fighting''—I winked confidently—''and that's how we're gonna 'proach this pickle you got into.''

''You sure?'' he asked, doubtful.

''Yup.''

You could tell he still couldn't believe it as he sloshed on that big flop hat of his and tipped it to Callie before leaving.

''You're not serious about this, are you?'' Callie said, worry coming to her face.

''She's right, you know,'' Robert threw in. ''It's madness!''

''Only one's gonna be mad is them Rebs when we get his wagons back from 'em.'' I smiled.

''But you can't—''

''Mister,'' I said as hard and even as I could make it, throwing a cock-eyed glance at him, ''how do you think I got to be this *old*?''

That shut him up, and I grabbed up Callie's trunk again and continued the walk I had started to make some two hours ago. Conversation sort of dried up like a Mojave waterhole until we got to the hotel—or what passed for it in this town—in the middle of the next block. But not even that turned out to be what it was supposed to be. This was just turning into one of those to-hell-and-gone days.

''Callie, I don't know what it is you females pack in these things, but you ought to get rid of at least half of it,'' I said, setting the trunk down beside the clerk's desk. ''Hell, a she-bear's cub weighs less'n this, half-growed!''

''Are you through being droll, sir?''

The clerk had that smart-ass look I never did care for in townfolk, the one that says they can't stand anyone who don't live permanent in their town. I bent over the desk, as if looking underneath it.

''What are you doing, sir?''

''Why, looking fer that dictionary and en-cyclopedia you got hereabouts. You can't be smart 'nough to think up a fancy word like that all by yourself.''

"You're trying my patience, *sir*."

This could go on all day, but I had better things to do.

"I was in here couple days back. Made a reservation for my sister for today. Paid up in full."

"I'm sorry, sir, but that room has been taken." Have you ever gotten the notion to flatten somebody just because you didn't like the attitude they had toward you? Well, if you have, friend, you know just how I was feeling then. Blood starts crawling up the back of your neck real slow, and even if the other fellow doesn't know it, you've got a lit fuse.

"Taken?" It was likely the most polite thing I'd said all day.

"See for yourself." You'd think he owned the place the way he turned that sign-in book around to face me. And sure as God made green apples there was the line I'd put my name on. Of course, it had been crossed out in three heavy black-inked lines, and another name placed above it. And that tore it!

"Mister, I've about had it with being treated like spit today," I said, bringing Mister Henry up and over the counter so the barrel rested on his chest. Now, some say it's the tone of my voice that scares the hell out of people, but I'd have wagered right then that it was the thought of dying that turned this fellow pale. "I paid up in full, sonny, so you already got my silver. If you don't put that name of mine back on your ledger right quick, you're going to be collecting some of my lead too!"

"But there's a man up there!"

"Believe me, pilgrim, he's going to be a lot easier to deal with than me. Guaranteed." The rifle barrel still rested on his chest.

"Well, I suppose I can talk to him. . . ."

"Let's do that," I said, easing the rifle up as he moved toward the stairs to the second floor.

Mama taught us the manners in the family, while Pa was the one who showed us how to keep meat on the fire and get along with nature instead of fighting her. Mama said it was always polite to knock before entering a room, but I'll tell you, hoss, I didn't care if it was Abe Lincoln in that room; by God, one way or another he was leaving!

It wasn't Abe Lincoln.

The door wasn't locked, and when I opened it the fellow who was supposedly using the room had the stink of a drunk about him and was passed out on the bed to prove it. I opened the window to air the place out.

"Come on, friend, time's up," I said, grabbing the lifeless body by the shirt and standing it upright. He wasn't dead yet, but if he drank any more of the stuff he smelled of he might get that way. Taos Lightning tends to kill you, cure you, or drive you blind. I patted him a couple times on the cheeks, but it was obvious this fellow wasn't anywhere to be found in this world, so I hoisted him over my shoulder, which was the equivalent of carrying Callie's trunk again, took him downstairs, and plunked him into a spare chair that looked like it was fairly well built. The smart-aleck clerk had followed my every step.

"I never did carry one of them fancy fob watches, mister, but I'd gauge you got upwards of half an hour before I expect that room to be ready for my sister." The clerk had lost some of his spunk in favor of what these townfolk call awe. That means they don't too often see us heathens do what I just did.

"Half an hour? But the woman who does the changing hasn't come in yet." It was plain to see he hadn't been treated like this by man nor beast in some time.

"I believe half an hour should be more than sufficient," Robert said as he pulled out a watch from his fob. I should have known.

I never did learn whether it was me or that honest-to-God timing piece that set that fellow in motion, but hell, I didn't really care as long as Callie got her room. It was twenty minutes by Robert's watch when the clerk was back downstairs, pleased as punch that he'd beat the time set for him.

"I made my bed better than that the first time Mama showed me how," I said in mild disgust as we entered the room. The breeze that had picked up had aired the room well, but those sheets and blanket were thrown onto the bed, at best. On the other hand, after lugging that trunk up those stairs you can bet I wasn't about to move it anywhere else for some time.

"I can fix it up, Ezra," Callie said, almost apologetically, "really, it's nothing."

The clerk made a quick exit as my sister set about straightening up what he hadn't. That seemed about the best time to say what I had to to Robert Carston so I gently took hold of his elbow and steered him back out to the hallway.

"Seems to me you can take care of yourself, if need be," I said, remembering what had happened earlier in the day and his actions.

"I always thought so." He said it matter-of-factly, not yet sure what it was I was getting at.

"Callie takes a shine to you, too."

"Well, I've taken a liking to her as well, Mister Hooker," he said shyly.

"I'm gonna be gone a couple of days, Robert, seeing if I can get that fella who helped out this morning back with his wagons where he belongs."

"Oh, I see." He brightened with a smile now. "And you'd like me to keep an eye on your sister while you're gone. Well, don't you worry, Mr. Hooker, she'll be in fine hands." He was about to walk back into the room, figuring our conversation was through, I reckon, when I laid a firm hand on his shoulder and stopped him about as stock-still in his tracks as a body can do to another.

"We got some right mean Injuns out here, Robert," I said. The glance I gave him then had more than a bit of concern in it. "Now, when they get to warring, why, they's all mean as hell, yes, sir. But the Blackfoot . . . why, they can be rattlesnake mean. I know 'cause John Colter said so. When they take you captive, you see, they get right testy, right testy.

"Fact is, they like to know how brave their captive is. Way they do that is to stake you down on the ground face up and do it."

"It?" He was getting a bit squeamish, but then most of those easterners do when you tell them this kind of story.

"Yup. They get a knife and start on one side and work their way over across your chest to the other side. Cut good long strips of your skin about an inch thick. Just a tad deep, mind you, for they don't want you to bleed to death afore they figure you're worth letting die quickly or not. Then, real slow like, they pull those strips of flesh off'n your chest one at a time. Brave man can stand the pain, won't utter so much as a word while they do it. Others, well, they say some of 'em is near mad afore that first strip is pulled clean off."

"Is there a reason for telling me this?" Robert asked softly, a little green at the gills. I'd had my hand on his shoulder all the time I'd told the story, but it was now I released it and planted it on my hip.

"Matter of fact there is, Robert." I was squinting now, the way you do when you want a body to know you can see right through any devious thing they might have in mind. "Callie seems to think you done a good job looking after her on that stage ride from back east, so I reckon I can trust you to do it for a couple more days. What you want to know, son, is that when I get back, well, if I find her any worse-for-the-wear"—here I smiled but there wasn't anything happy about it—"why, I'm gonna give you a personal demonstration of what I just described . . . 'cept *I'm* going to be the Blackfoot and *you're* going to be the captive. You get the drift of what I mean?"

He gulped hard. "I believe so."

"Good. I knew I could count on you."

I turned to go, but he said, "Black Jack," and this time it was me that was surprised.

"Yeah."

"The expression on that young man—Bill's—face . . . Why did he look that way when he said he was the only one who'd escaped?"

"There's a whole different set of values out here, I reckon. Most times you wander off with a pard, you figure he'll stand by you if you get twixt a rock and a hard place.

Mought be you send him for help or t'other way 'round
and only you and him know it. Them that don't know the
situation tend to judge you by their own values.'' I
shrugged. ''Times it ain't right, but that's the way it is.''

''Do you really think you'll be able to get those—''

''Bill, he'll get his wagons back,'' I interrupted. ''You
take my word for it, that boy's dangerous. It's the silent
ones you learn to watch out for.''

''Silent ones?'' As puzzled as he looked, I figured Robert had a lot to learn about this land and its people.

''Grizzly bear's big, Robert, and he makes one helluva
noise. Gila monster, on the other hand, he ain't but a foot
and a half long and ain't got no bite a'tall.'' I smiled, then
winked at him. ''But if he grabs a chunk of you in his
mouth, why, you're as sure dead as if that griz had taken
your head off. You think on that.''

And I left.

Chapter 3

Civilized or not, most towns know they do just as much if not more business *after* daylight hours as they do during. Nighttime it's usually the saloons that get the business profits. Just before daybreak . . . well, unless you're in the habit of burning daylight out here, it's the eateries that make a small fortune about then. Next time you hear about some gold or silver strike that's sure to make you rich overnight, hoss, forget about investing in a pickax and a sluice pan; hell, it was likely the fella working the general store who started the rumor anyway. You want to make some money, you find the location of that strike and open up an eatery of sorts, preferably with a woman doing the cooking. Man's always got to eat, and if you've got a decent-looking woman serving up the food, why, the customers likely won't pay any attention to how good or bad the food tastes, as long as they can take a gander once in a while at that woman serving it.

"Annie's" was the name of the place I found the next morning about an hour before sunup. I do believe she was built near twice as thick as me, but Lordy, could she cook! I waited some before I got a seat but it was worth it. She served up a couple good slices of beef, along with eggs and spuds and strong, black coffee, and you can bet I ate every bit of it. If Bill was going to lead me where I thought we were going, we weren't going to have time for much of a noon camp unless it was to rest the horses.

When Bill walked in you'd have thought the whole place was going to clear out then and there. But then, if you'd been one of the mob that got stood off yesterday, you might be giving serious thought to leaving the territory, too, if you saw Bill walk into Annie's with his own two pistols stuck in his waistband, butts forward, and two more in hand. That was a man who was ready for war, friend, and I had the feeling that most folks thereabouts knew more about that than I did.

Apparently, Annie was the only one not afraid of Bill as she brought an empty cup to the table and poured coffee. There'd been at least three others sharing the table with me, but they vacated the area right quick. Too bad Robert wasn't there to see it; he'd have known what I meant about this man being dangerous if he was.

"Darlin'," I said to Annie as she refilled my cup, "you set a fine table. Five, ten minutes you can tell them yahoos in the corner over there they can have it back. Whenever I'm in this neck of the woods, you'll have my business for sure." I winked at her, and she blushed some before leaving.

"Quite the lady's man." Bill smiled.

"Not hardly. Just conforming to Pappy's rules."

"Pappy's rules?"

"Course! Always stay on the good side of the cook, son. Man don't have to have a helluva lot of friends to get through life, but you shouldn't pass up a good meal, 'cause everybody's gotta eat."

Like I said, we had a ways to go before daybreak, and we had a jump on the rest of the world as we rode out of town. Bill had a couple more pistols inside an interesting piece of leather he'd thrown over the back of his saddle. When I asked, he said it was a version of the mochila the Pony Express riders had carried the mail in a few years back, this one being a bit enlarged so he could fit those Army and Navy Colts in it. Not a bad idea, I thought, as we rode out, remembering that for years I'd been carrying my possibles in a war bag just like the old mountain men did.

Missouri is nothing like anything else God ever created; of course, I said the same thing about the Shinin' Mountains when I first saw them. I reckon men feel like that wherever they go; seeing things for the first time leaving the impression it does on a body. Mind you, I've been across what they call "The Great American Desert," an area which isn't really desert at all—it just looked that way to Pike and Long when they made their first ventures into it. There are stretches of flatland where I'd swear you could see a hundred miles to your front, and those Rockies, why, I never do think I'll have the time to find out how far north or south they go—mister, they just *go* for as far as you can see! But this Missouri, why it was a combination of both flat and rugged and sawed-off at the knees to boot! You can ride across some flatland for a ways and then come to land that rolls so far up and down you'd think you were at the base of a small mountain. Why, I'm surprised a flash flood hasn't taken it all away by now!

It was that land we traveled through that morning, heading back to the place where Bill said he'd lost his wagons and men. He was quiet nearly all the time, and when we did find the spot, no one had to tell us what to do. It seemed automatic for us to circle the area and see if there had been any sign left to pick up so we could track the bastards down. Bill found it finally and gave a whistle. We decided to give the horses a rest, first. It was close enough to noon to make a dry camp before setting out to do some serious tracking.

"You ain't much on pistols, are you?" he said after a few bites of beef jerky.

"I could say the same to you 'bout long guns." I took a swallow from my canteen. "Nope, pistols never did give me comfort."

"I noticed this morning."

"Mister Henry here will do me fine."

"Mister Henry?"

I shrugged. "When you get to being alone for as long as I have, son, I reckon you find your own conversations to carry on."

"Some of them folks back there," he said, throwing a thumb over his shoulder, "they figure if you do that, you must be crazy."

"Shoot, boy, if I *didn't* do it, I'd be crazy!" I hefted the rifle in my hands. "No, sir, thank you, but this Henry will do me fine."

"Heard some about it. Uses those new metallic cartridges, don't it?" Bill asked.

"Yup."

"Ain't gonna last, you know. A fad is what they're saying it is. Percussion's here to stay." He seemed confident about what he was saying.

"Could be, lad, but until they stop making ammunition for this model, I do believe I'll stick with it."

I'd been brought up on an old flintlock Pappy had. Hell, it was the *only* gun he had! The percussion cap came into use just before Ashley and Henry went to the Shinin' Mountains, and the first decent gun it was used on was the Hawken. I'd carried one of them for years, and it was a right fine long gun. Only reason I gave it up was because after the mountain men came all those pilgrims wanting to settle any- and everywhere they could, making the Indians madder than hell in the process. Then the war started, and I had people from all over shooting my way before I had a chance to identify myself. That was when I rode into civilization for the first time in a long time and wound up trading in my Hawken for a brand new Henry rifle.

The clerk in that store knew his firearms and gave me a short history of what he called the Henry Lever-Action Cartridge Magazine Rifle. A new kind of repeater rifle is what it was, but those folks back east that make all this hardware we use out here; well, I reckon they want to make sure you know exactly what it is you're getting. B. Tyler Henry was who it was named after and he worked out of an outfit known as the New Haven Repeating Arms Company. What this Henry fellow did, it seems, was improve on something called the Jennings rifle—whatever that was—and he came out with a lever action that enabled you to shoot, reload, and fire all of fifteen .44 caliber rounds as fast as you could, and pard, after using that Hawken all those years . . . well, that was some shooting! Fact is, if you were nimble with your fingers and could reload fast enough, you could fire all of thirty rounds in one minute's time! You had to reload from the bottom of the receiver, feeding the rounds into a tubular magazine that stretched the full length of the twenty-four-inch barrel, but considering that all you had to do was pull that lever down about ninety degrees to eject the used cartridge, cock the hammer, and prime yourself for the next shot, well, hoss, you got no complaint from me. No, sir. Not even for the nine and a half pounds it weighed.

"You say it was Rebs who took your wagons?" I asked, screwing the cap back on the canteen and getting to my feet.

"Yeah, why?"

We mounted up.

"Just crossed my mind." Sometimes you can tell when folks are trying to read your thoughts just from the look about you, and I reckon Bill was doing that now, the curious glance he gave me.

"Oh?"

"Yeah." I smiled. "Heard a Rebel the other day, discussing guns with his amigos. Called the Henry 'that damned Yankee rifle that you can load on Sunday and fire all week.' "

Bill smiled soft-like. "So?"

"Them fellas we're going after have got a real surprise in store for 'em." I slapped my hand to the large pockets of the buckskin jacket I wore to make him aware of the extra cartridges that I carried. Then I smiled and gave him that mischievous look again. "You give me enough ammunition, son, and Mister Henry can do my talking for all of a *month*."

We tracked them north, but just like I thought, they doubled back and headed south by west on us. Not that they were all that hard to track, mind you. Hell, how are you going to cover the tracks of two or three freight wagons, even when they're only half-loaded? No, it wasn't hard to track them at all.

It was late afternoon when I spotted what was likely those Rebs in the distance, and reined in.

"How many you figure they was in the party that attacked you?" I asked, squinting as I counted the number of mounts I could see.

"Twenty-five, thirty, I'd say," Bill replied, doing the same counting.

"I'd say half of 'em's gone. What's your figure?"

"You called it right, Hooker." I never could figure out why it is people do or don't call you by your name. It must be something to do with whether they want or don't want to be friendly toward you, I reckon. This was the first time Bill Whatever-His-Name-Was had addressed me as anything, and it got my curiosity up.

Next thing you know he was checking the loads of those Colts of his; me doing the same with my Henry and the pair of pistols I was toting as well. It didn't strike me until I pushed those pistols back in my belt that it wasn't even dark yet and here we were, getting ready for war.

"Say, just what is it you got in mind, son?" I never was too keen on flat-out charging into hell, at least not without a bucket of water or so.

"I don't know about you, mister, but I'm getting ready to get my wagons back." Now, that ain't the sanest thing I ever did hear a man say, but I'll give him credit for being to the point about it. Not bright, but to the point.

"Just like that."

He nodded. "Just like that." His face wasn't soft, anymore, nor his voice. It was the same crossness, the same danger that had come out in him yesterday; I could have been along for the ride for all he cared just then.

"Well, now," I said, giving him a dose of how I feel when some young pup decides he's going to boss the expedition, "be that as it is, I do believe I'll have a say in just how it is I'm about to lose my hide."

"Then be quick about it. I've more and better things to do." Pure business, he was. A real doer.

"In a hurry to get yourself killed, are you." I said it more as a statement than a question. "Or are you just seeing if you can make me riled up enough to get killing mad as you?" It wouldn't be the first time a man was ever challenged about whether or not he had the sand to get something done, just so it *would* get done.

"Old man." He drew it out, impatient like, the way I'd seen these *civilized* townfolk do when talking to an oldtimer they thought to be senile or addled. Bill was sitting a-saddle to my left, which didn't make it hard at all to put the right sort of hitch in my elbow so that Mister Henry was resting in the crook of my arm, pointed right at his head.

"You tone yourself down right quick, sonny, or when I ride into that camp it'll be alone, and the only thing you're gonna be charging is that patch of ground on your left side." He wasn't one to shake easy, I'll say that for him, but he knew I meant as much business as he did now and no question about it.

"You wouldn't." The caution in him was coming out now, and if he was smart, he was turning into a believer real quick.

"Believe me, son, you don't want to listen to me sit here and tell you how much I'd like to do it." I paused, gave him a serious squint and a frown to go along with it. "Just take my word for it."

"All right, I apolo—"

"No, what you want to do, lad, is listen." I eased the hammer forward on the Henry gently, although the weapon was still aimed at its original target. "You think you can do that?"

"Sure." I thought I detected a sigh. "Didn't mean to—"

"Just listen, remember? *Listen.*" Biggest thing this boy was going to have to learn was patience, unless I missed my guess.

"As I recollect, me and Gar Hanson run into a similar situation back in the spring of '34 . . . or mebbe it was '35. It was the rendezvous where Marcus Whitman pulled that arrow out of Bridger's back. Had it there for two years, he had. Discombobulated the good doctor, it purely did." I smiled, remembering the event.

"Anyway, Gar and me was the only ones saved our hair when those Blackfoot overrun us and took our pelts and a handful of horses. Prime horses, prime pelts. Killed one of our group and took the rest prisoners." I shivered, then, seeing in my mind the sight of the young lad they had staked out, naked as the day he was born, when we tracked our way to that Blackfoot camp. Hadn't been for his screams, I do believe we'd never have found it. They'd stripped away three or four slices of flesh from his chest. That was how I could detail such a thing to Robert Carston. The whole incident flooded my memory for an instant.

"There was more blood in that camp than you've ever seen, son." I winced, then, the way you do when you're reliving something terrible from the past like that. "Poor Danny." My voice was soft, now, remembering the screams that wouldn't stop. "Had to do away with him."

"Lost a horse?"

"Huh? Oh, yeah, a horse. Yeah, that's it."

"You mean just the two of you went into that camp and got all your things back?" Bill asked in disbelief.

"That we did."

"But how? It couldn't have been a whole Blackfoot camp."

"More like these pilgrims we're a-chasing. Dozen or so in a temporary camp, just making their way back to the main wickiup with their plunder. Diversion, that's the fancy word for what we set up; that's how we got in there and did what we did." I wasn't about to tell him about how young Daniel and his screams not only gave away their location, but enabled us to surprise and bloody them as much as we did.

"You figure on doing that here? Just waltzing into camp and taking it over?" Bill asked.

"Don't tell me you're losing your gumption, son. First it was a fandango you was wanting to start, now it's a waltz."

"No, Hooker, there ain't nothing wrong with—"

"First thing you're going to do, son, is get rid of that flop hat of yours." The look he gave me was pure defiance, but he wasn't as pushy with me now as before; his pushiness he could save for those yahoos in the camp.

"They might not have recognized you in the heat of that raid, Bill, but that woolsey you're sporting is a one of a kind," I told him.

He took it off grudgingly, but after looking around a bit he found a shrub of sorts and tossed the hat onto it.

"Least the snakes won't get into it," he said.

"Son, I got a feeling that if a diamondback bit you right now, why, he'd die of being poisoned." Saying that didn't make the situation any easier, but I had a notion it took the edge off of Bill some. "Let's go," I added and reined to the right.

"Wait a minute! They're—"

"You give that mount its head and walk it along, and I'll let you know what we're going to do."

If we were going to ride into camp and come out alive, we were going to have to create a diversion, for there wasn't a young boy named Danny screaming his lungs out to draw attention away from us this time. What I had in mind was circling to the west side of camp and riding in with the sun at our backs, as it was getting to be late afternoon now, anyway. It wasn't much, but shaving the odds as much in our favor as possible was what counted now— along with getting out alive.

"And what is it you've got in mind once we reach the camp?" Bill asked.

"Well, since everyone's so interested in how feeble-minded I am, I figured I'd just act like an old man."

He shook his head in disbelief, the way a fellow does when he's telling himself that he can't win for losing and there isn't much he can do about it to boot.

It must have taken close to an hour to get there, slow as our horses were walking, but we made it. The greeting was about as friendly as you might expect in those days—half a dozen of them came out as a welcoming committee, as armed to the teeth as we were.

"Friendly bunch," I said aloud to no one in particular. They looked about as mean as I figured the lad I was riding with felt.

"Passing through," Bill added. "Thought we might get some directions."

"Don't josh me, mister," a gruff-looking hombre replied. He wore a couple of scars here and there but he was still a young buck trying to act more than his age.

"Tell me something, sonny," I said, squinting down at him out of the corner of one eye, "was you born a bastard or do you just work at it natural?" For some reason, the youngsters fighting that war seemed to think that if you outnumbered the other fellow, he was supposed to automatically be scared or something, so my comment threw him. While he was thinking it over, I glanced at Bill and added, "Must be both."

Come to think of it, Bill didn't look any too happy about what I'd said, either. But what can you expect from an old man, right?

"Seen you coming for an hour now, old man," another said. "You'd have a hard time making me believe that you come for directions, old man."

" 'Twasn't me came for directions," I said, nodding my head to Bill. "He's the one who asked." The way Bill was looking, he either figured I was overdoing my crazy-old-man part or had become convinced that I *was* a crazy old man. To make it even more convincing, I threw a squinty eye at him along with one of my nastier looks and added, "Can't tell these young pups anything these days."

"What about your partner?" the first man asked.

"You mean that fella in the flop hat back yonder?" I said, looking past them back to the bush Bill had thrown his hat on. From the ground that bush could well have looked like a man, although all that was visible to me was that flop hat of Bill's. "Let's just say I got tired of riding double and came for a horse ary you got one. That fella back there, well, I told him if I ain't out of here in half an

hour or he hears some shooting . . . one of you fellas is
gonna die of lead poisoning. Got him a Sharps, he does.''

The Sharps had been around for more than a decade
now, having the reputation of being Old Reliable and particularly deadly at long ranges. Even if you couldn't see
the man but knew he had a Sharps, you held a certain
knowledge that you might well die not knowing who it was
that pulled the trigger. Now, hoss, that's usually the way
it happens, but no man wants to think about that sort of
death, and these youngsters weren't any different.

I dismounted slow, like a cranky old man is supposed to
do, taking note that the wagons were off to the left rear
and that a handful of men were seated against the side of
one, tied up by the looks of them. They would be Bill's
drivers. The other three men guarding them had taken a
sudden notion to glance back at that flop hat. I'd made sure
I'd spoken loud enough for the whole camp to hear what I
had to say about the man with the Sharps.

I had the whole show to myself as I walked toward the
wagons and the far side of the camp. You'd have thought
I was one of those ''Noble Redmen'' Tom Jefferson had
paraded in front of everyone back east and then in Europe.
Or maybe they were admiring my guts. One thing for sure,
it wasn't my buckskins that attracted their attention.

''Hey, where you going, old man?'' I don't know which
one said it, but there was a bit of panic in his voice.

''Don't worry about him,'' Bill said. Sometimes you can
hear someone talking and know that he's laughing at the
same time. Bill was doing it now. ''He's crazy as a loon.
Been up in the mountains too long. Keeps talking about
Bridger and Fitzpatrick and the rest of them. If you ask
me, he left a good part of him there.'' I wouldn't argue
that with him, not one bit. But this wasn't the time for
conversation. I kept on walking.

''All right, mister, but you'd better be quick about asking those directions. You're making me nervous. And take
your friend with you,'' I heard the first man say.

The whole time I was walking, I had the feeling my
backside was being watched by the entire camp. If you've

ever had the hair on your neck stick out and you knew there wasn't a lightning bolt in the entire territory, well, friend, you know exactly how I was feeling then. There was pure silence as I approached the wagons and started acting curious about their contents. Then Bill began palavering about his directions, getting the attention of at least some of these yahoos.

"Well, now," I said, giving a casual glance to the drivers tied up on the ground, "looks like you lads got yourselves in a peck of trouble." None said anything, eyeing me as suspiciously as the Rebs had. "Caught 'em stealing your goods, did you?" I asked one of the guards. Did you ever notice how some folks will accept a ready-made story you feed them, if it tends to suit their purpose, even when it's a lie?

"Yeah," the guard growled, throwing a killing glance at the men on the ground. "Damn Yanks is worse'n anything I ever seen in my life." An evil glare wasn't all he gave them, for the prisoner nearest me soon had tobacco juice on his shirt front.

"Well, son, you can keep your war. I don't want no part of it. Shoot, it's hard enough surviving on the frontier without having to fight everyone else's battles, too."

By that time I had my bowie out and was leaning over the side of the wagon, prying loose the lid of one of the boxes it held. That had the effect I wanted, for the guard reached over to grab me by the shirt sleeve, yanking my arm away as he did. Normally, mind you, I would have broken this kid's nose and a few other bones, but being a crazy old man I let him have his way, even helped him some when I let loose the bowie in midair and it went flying a good dozen feet behind me.

"Leave it alone, old man!" This boy was trying to prove he could be downright mean when he wanted to.

"All right, all right," I said in that meek way us crazy old men are supposed to act. After all, we're over the hill, right? Lordy, I thought, is it going to surprise this lad when he sees me coming back over that hill. "Say, son, you think you could fetch that for me?" I rolled one shoulder and cringed as the bones in it made an audible sound. There was no faking that; you get that way after a while if you fool around with Mother and Father. Mother Nature and Father Time, that is. "Pains me to bend over," I explained.

Cussing and moaning and groaning is what he did as he took his time going over to the knife. I swear, youngsters today won't do nothing for you without being asked or told first! That was when I squatted down quick like and took to examining the wagon wheel.

"You fellas better get as crampish as a young sailor his first time asea real quick like. Your rolling over's 'bout the only way I'm gonna get a chance to cut you loose." I said it as low as I could without being heard by anyone else.

The Yank nearest me was about to say something when the guard strode back with my bowie. I was still hunkered down, looking at the wheel.

"Here you are, old man." He handed me the knife.

I took it and then the drivers began moaning that their stomachs ached. I gave the guard a look of surprise.

"It's that damned water," one of the drivers said. "Putrid it was, I'll say that."

"Water?" the guard replied. "The water ain't brackish. It's—"

Everything happened at once then. But that's usually the way of it. Bill must have gotten directions to everywhere in the Missouri territory before those yahoos realized that he didn't have a top piece and the one yonder was likely his. That guard, well, I could see it had finally hit him that for all the aches and pains I'd complained about, I'd squatted down and gotten back up again as easy as could be.

Bill had both pistols out before I could see what had happened, shooting with both hands while his mount reared up, and doing a right fine job of hitting his targets as he did so. That being the only gunfire in camp at the time, it got all the attention, which gave me a quick second to do what I needed to.

I backhanded the guard, sending him reeling against one of the wagons, and followed it by bringing the butt of the handle of my bowie across his jaw and putting him to rest for a while.

In the meantime, the drivers had rolled to their sides, the rope tying their hands behind their backs being their only bonds. I cut two of them loose with one swift slash each and handed them the pistols in my belt. They made a scramble for cover as I cut the bonds of the second two, and one of them grabbed up the rifle and pistol of the guard I'd knocked unconscious.

Mister Henry was leaning against the wagon wheel where I'd left him. I was making my way to get hold of him when splinters from the wagon started flying as thick as the lead. For that matter, it was getting right breezy around my top-knot, for it looked like I was the center of attraction again.

You'd have thought we were gone beaver, going up against those kind of odds, but of a sudden those Rebel lads were scampering for their horses. Oh, they were still throwing lead, mind you, but they weren't mounting any vicious attack like the kind I'd heard had been fought back east. They were just mounting!

Could be it was that we'd evened up the odds some with five armed men behind two of the wagons. Or maybe it was the sight of those three dead bodies lying where Bill had started the shooting. Whatever it was, these boys were getting right cautious.

I shot one of them in the leg as he and a pard were getting ready to ride. The gunfire was now directed toward the five of us. I levered another shell into Mister Henry, glancing toward Bill's position. What I saw, well, mad wasn't the word for how it made me feel!

"I knew it! Damn it, I knew it," I all but yelled. There was Bill, riding hell-for-leather away from us! Sometimes you misjudge a man, but it's a damn shame when your life's depending on it! "Lousy son of a—"

"Do you know who you're talking about?" one driver asked, a look of astonishment crossing his face before a hail of gunfire brought the battle alive to him again.

"I don't give a damn if he is your boss!" I said and

fired three more rounds into a third wagon these yahoos had taken to hiding behind.

Fact is, they had seen Bill leave, and except for the three or four who had taken off, the rest were now deciding to stay and fight. Damn him, anyway!

I reckon that was when these Johnny Rebs came on to what I was hoping wouldn't cross their minds until after they'd run off. That being that there weren't any reloads for the cap-and-ball pistols the drivers had. No one said anything just then, but I got some serious looks that only had one question behind them: *How in the hell are we going to get out of this mess?*

I've never been afraid to admit to being scared; staying that way in a tight spot has helped me get out of more than one of them in my lifetime. Trouble is that just admitting it doesn't solve the problem, and it was looking like staying alive was about to turn into a real serious problem here. Yes, sir. I had no idea of whether these drivers were the kind to cut and run, like their boss had, or if they would stand and fight to the last, but I'll tell you, friend, shoving those reloads into Mister Henry got me to wondering. Those Rebs had a hungry look about them that said they were going to mount an attack and be damned to us.

"If you boys got religion, I'd advise you to get right close to it 'bout now," I said as the Rebels gathered for a charge. "I already met Ezekiel oncet and I know where I'm going when I die."

I had a notion they were about to walk out on me, then and there. But they didn't.

Like I said, sometimes you misjudge a man.

At the same time those yahoos charged us, Bill came riding back into camp. I don't know where the reins of his horse were, but I can tell you he had two pistols in his hands, and from the fire coming out of those barrels, you can believe he was dishing out hell in large amounts. Me, I did the same thing with Mister Henry, making three of those horses riderless by the time they got close to the wagon. That kind of firepower broke their spirit and it wasn't long before the survivors were heading for the open spaces and as much horizon as they could cover on their mounts.

"Right handy with them short guns," I said. "But it took you long enough to reload."

"I didn't." I gave him a hard look that said I didn't quite believe him. "When I ran out of ammunition, I took off after that horse of yours, Hooker. It was the only one that had any guns on it ready to fire." Then I remembered the two pistols I'd put in my slicker and war bag. "Why, give you some doubt, did I!" he asked.

This time he was the one demanding the whole truth.

"Oh, no," I said, like the experienced storyteller I was. "Just biding our time, we was, and waiting for you to start the ball."

"You mean this old coot is the only one you brought back with you to get us out of this scrape?" one of the drivers said. "We could have been killed!"

"Man's got a point," Bill said, looking to me for an answer. "The way you were acting when we rode in, I figured we were dead for sure."

"Not hardly! Told you this is how old Gar and me pulled it off with them Blackfoot."

"Oh?"

"Sure! Works every time! Walk into your enemy's camp, show him the cheek of one side of your ass and dare him to kick the other and apply the golden rule while he's a-thinking it over."

"The golden rule?" he asked. Let me tell you, I had these boys mystified more than a medicine man at a war council.

"Yup. Do unto others *afore* they do unto you."

Chapter 4

It looked like one of those bloody battles I'd been hearing about back east, just on a smaller scale. There were eight of them laying there dead and deposits of blood in as many other places in the area.

"There's shovels in one of these wagons, boys," Bill said, "better start looking for 'em. We got some burying to do."

All but one of the four men did what he was told. The last just stood there with Bill and me, mostly staring at me, though.

"You didn't really come all the way out here, knowing what you'd be up against, just to save our hides, did you?" he asked.

"Well, your boss here saved my skin yesterday. Weren't for him, I'd likely have gotten my hide tanned, so you might say I owed him one."

"Never had any second thoughts?" Bill said, and I couldn't tell if it was an honest question or he was starting up trouble again.

"Oh . . . oncet," I said. I never have made an awful lot of friends in this lifetime, but I'll guarantee you one thing, hoss, no one ever has any doubts about what I feel about anything. You don't make the same amount of friends being honest that politicking would get you, but you generally manage to get a good bit of respect—and I've taught both my boys that line of thought, too. "When I seen you light a shuck out of here, I figured you might be heading for the hills." I swallowed hard. "I was wrong about that, Bill. Wrong about you."

I can count on the fingers of one hand the number of times I've ever apologized to anyone in my life, and most of them were to my wife a long time ago. This was about as close as you'd ever get me to saying I was sorry to a man on this frontier. I think Bill knew that.

"But you stayed anyway?" the driver asked, a bit in awe.

"Had to. One thing that tends to wear out on a man is his legs, and as pained as mine get these days, why, I couldn't run if I wanted to, so I just stand and fight and hope I've got enough ammunition.

"Then there's this." I picked up my now ventilated beaver hat, which had holes on the east and west sides where the bullet had gone through. "One of them sorry bastards put a hole in my war bonnet and that made me mad."

"You mean you got into this oversized fandango over a hat!" the driver said.

"Son, do you know how hard it is to find one of these pesky little critters up there in the Shinin' Mountains?" I asked, holding the hat up to him. "Why, there ain't hardly enough of 'em to mate in the spring to keep the population going."

Bill was standing off to the side, now, enjoying the show.

"He's crazy!" the man said to him before stomping off to join the others.

I shrugged. "There's them that say I am and then there's them that . . . well, some of 'em just don't say."

At least Bill had a sense of humor, for he was getting a laugh out of all this. Me, well, I had a couple questions of my own.

"By the by, son," I said, "in the heat of all this fighting, one of your compadres asked me if I knew *who* you were. The fact that I didn't was sort of embarrassing, considering that it's you wanted to start this war. Now, just in case we have to do this all over again, you don't mind my asking now, so I can give the right answer when they ask again, do you?''

''I told you yesterday, it's Bill.'' Judging from the look on his face, I'd say he was getting about as edgy as he had been before we'd taken on these Rebs.

''Most everyone I know's got at least two names,'' I said, pushing it. ''Seems about the only thing in this world you can't blame a man for.''

''All right. Bill Barnes. That suit you?'' Now, friend, if he didn't say that grudgingly, I'm uglier than Aunt Sarah, and you'd have to go some to beat that.

''Just curious.''

''Well, keep that bit of curiosity to yourself, Hooker, and especially that name.'' He said it in that same soft voice of his, but it was hard underneath, no mistaking it.

The graves were shallow, covered by what few rocks and such we could fine in the area, and would doubtless be dug up by the coyotes and feasted upon by buzzards and others who survived on dead meat, but we made fast work of it and had all of those Rebs planted by the time the sun had been down an hour. By then, Bill Barnes had turned into as much of a hard case as some of those loud-mouths we'd put away. Hard to figure, this one.

''Bill, you want to put up a grave marker or something?'' one of the drivers asked from the shadows. ''I know we don't know any of their names, but the boys were just thinking. . . . .'' He let it trail off, but there was no denying that every word had been said in caution. I wondered, then, who *was* this man I was sharing the fire with?

''Don't make any difference to me,'' Bill said. ''Do what you like. You just put down that they stole from the wrong man at the wrong time.'' Then he tossed the remains of his coffee onto the ground and walked out into the night.

Fitful is how my sleep gets once in a while. There are times when exhaustion carries you right through the night and you wake up in the same position you lay down in and it seems like you just closed your eyes. Other nights your memory gets overworked; the past catching up with your mind is how one back-easterner explained it once. That night was full of the past for me; it was Danny and Gar and me and those Blackfoot Indians all over again, just like it had been a hundred times before.

"Mister, you sure get noisy at night," one of the drivers said while the coffee boiled the next morning.

"Oh?" I could feel the red crawling up the back of my neck again. It was times like this I was glad I had a full growth of whiskers.

"Yeah, you called out for Danny a couple times, whoever he is. I swear they could've heard you two counties over."

"Old Hooker, he's a horse lover," Bill said unexpectedly. "Told me he lost a horse by that name some years back in the mountains. Ain't that what you said?" It threw me some, for this wasn't the callous man who'd walked off into the night the evening before, not a'tall. The way he was cocking his eye at me, I'd a feeling he'd heard me during the night, too. Fact is, I had the notion he knew Danny wasn't a horse as well as I did. Yeah, he knew.

"That's a fact," I said, and that was the end of it.

We broke camp and Bill and his lads got their wagons ready to complete the trip they'd yet to finish. None of the supplies were missing, so his plan was to go ahead with his schedule, late as he was.

While they were breaking camp I went through the half dozen horses that the Rebs had left behind; a black roan and a feisty mustang that looked to have bottom to it being the two I picked. The saddles weren't all that good, but that didn't matter for what I had in mind.

"What are you doing now?" Bill asked as I saddled up, the horses in tow.

"Maybe asking directions was just your way of stretching the blanket with those Rebs yesterday, son, but when I said I came for horses, that's just what I meant. My sis and that fella with her are gonna be needing mounts for the traveling we've got ahead of us, and I figure these will do."

He didn't say any more about it; either not wanting to make more trouble or not caring, one. "Thanks for the

help, Hooker. You came along at the right time and I'm
obliged.''

I reckon he figured that was the end of it, for he turned
to go back to his wagons and men. Well, it wasn't quite
finished, not for me, anyway.

''Actually,'' I said, loud enough to stop him in his tracks
and make him turn and take notice of me again, ''there's
one other reason I come along on this war party.''

''Oh?'' Like it or not I had his attention now.

''Yeah. You young bucks keep needing to be reminded
that if it wasn't for us old, senile coots, you'd never make
it in this land.'' Bill seemed taken aback over that statement. ''Hell, somebody's gotta teach you how!''

''You think I need to be taught how to make it?''

''Well, mebbe not how,'' I conceded. ''But it sure
seemed like you needed a lesson in how an old bastard like
me still knows what to do.'' The beginning of a smile was
building on his face now. ''You mark my words, son, ten,
fifteen years from now you'll be saying the same thing.''

The smile was complete now. ''Really?''

''Guaranteed.''

He turned again to leave.

''Bill.''

''Yeah,'' he said over his shoulder.

''About this morning.'' I paused, clearing my throat.
''Thanks.''

That was the end of it, so I rode on back to Independence.

Chapter 5

Like I said, women will be the death of me yet.

When I got back to Independence, Robert Carston was still cautiously friendly toward me—hell, maybe he took that Blackfoot story serious—but Callie had changed some. Not the way she looked, mind you, but the *way* she looked . . . if you know what I mean. Why, I've seen jaybirds in the middle of a spring thunder boomer that looked about as carefree as she did when I rode up in front of that hotel. I hadn't yet stopped by the livery to drop off the horses and I was digging in a pocket for some silver or gold when she came bursting out of that front door.

"Ezra!" she said, just like she had the day I'd met her on the coach, and I winced again just like I had then. But she was happy to see me, no doubt about that.

"Son," I said, looking at a nine-year-old with hungry eyes who'd spotted me entering town and had walked with me and my mounts all the way to where we now stood, "how 'bout you take these three horses down to the livery and have the man feed 'em good and rub 'em down. They been a far piece." I handed him the two coins. "This'n's for the liveryman and this'n's yours." I winked at him, smiling. "Don't get sick on it."

"Yes, sir." Even the money didn't faze him, for he seemed awestruck, like he was seeing Bridger in the flesh or some other hero he'd heard about. But maybe he knew I was part of a dying breed, the same as those beaver that

44

had long since become scarce. Sometimes these young ones can tell more than you think.

"You're bound and determined to get me into a fight, ain't you, calling me by that name of mine," I said to Callie. But not even the half-serious frown I gave her could shake that smile.

"I have to talk to you, Ez—" she stammered, pulling her head out of the sky at least long enough to correct herself. "I have to talk to you, *brother*," she said, before all but dragging me inside.

"Saw Robert on the way into town," I said, wondering what I was getting into now. "Seems in high spirits. Says you're doing right well. 'Pears he's right."

It was up in her room that the fireworks started, or maybe I should say the waterworks. I hadn't set Mister Henry down before she came to me and kissed me on what part of a cheek she could find under all that growth . . . and busted out in tears, hanging onto me for dear life as she did.

"Careful now, hon," I said in as soft a voice as Bill's, "you keep this up and you're gonna rust Mister Henry." When it didn't get any dryer on my chest I dropped the war bag and tossed Mister Henry onto the bed, taking her in my arms. Holding her reminded me of Martha the time she hurt, but that was long ago. When the tears subsided, I worked my way over to the bed and slowly set her down on it.

"Last time I recall you crying was when I left," I said, going through the war bag, finally finding what I was after. The red bandana I kept rolled up with some of my medicinals was likely the only clean thing I had. "Only I ain't leaving now, that I know of. Hell, sis, you and me got a far piece of traveling to do. Here, dry up your eyes," I said and handed her the kerchief.

"It's hard telling if you're angelliferous happy or downright exfluctuated," I went on. And that was the truth! She didn't appear any the worse for wear physically; no, what was bothering her was on the inside, the part of a woman no man ever sees and can never second-guess. After more silence, I added, "You know, Callie, I've always had a notion about women. The fickle ones are like a careless man with a gun; they're both likely to hurt someone. Course, I never did figure you for fickle."

That did it.

"I love him, Ezra," she said through swollen eyes. "Robert. I love him."

"But you don't hardly know him!" I must have sounded like a mother hen, but you've got to remember that courting took a while in those days. Why, I remember when Martha and me . . .

"But I *do* know him, Ezra!" she said in defense. "We spent two weeks on the stagecoach together. Oh, Ezra, he's bright and warm and educated—"

"Got tarnational little horse sense, if you ask me. Why, he . . ." I stopped then and there as it hit me. "Say, wait a minute. If you're in love with him and he's so all-fired great, well . . . why are you crying?"

A couple new tears started rolling down her cheeks.

"I'm not sure if he loves me or not," she said, and that kerchief of mine got another good soaking. Fact is, if it had been anyone else, any other woman, I'd likely have told her to do her crying in the garden where the water wouldn't be wasted—there was precious little of it, as it was, on this frontier. But what could I do; she was my sister.

"Don't you worry, Callie," I said, patting her shoulder, "it'll all work out. Robert, he just needs time is all." He was going to have until sundown to think it over, if I had my way; otherwise, he'd better be out of town by the next sunrise.

"Are you sure?"

"You bet, hon." I grabbed up Mister Henry. "I'm gonna check the livery to see if that boy got my mounts took care of proper. You find yourself that fancified dress you was wearing on the coach and dig it out. Trail meat ain't cooked near as well as the steaks in some of the eateries these civilized towns got."

"Ezra?" she said when I'd reached the door.

"Yeah."

"You're not going to force him, are you? You're not going to start a fight over this, are you? You know how I—"

"Now, Callie, you know good and well I never go out of my way to look for a fight." I said it with as straight a face as I could, closing the door behind me as I did so, for if I gave her a chance to reply, I knew I'd never hear the end of it.

I found him about a block away, just past the saloon, heading in my direction. He started to give me a greeting, but I pushed him into a half-right turn and had him up against the wall with Mister Henry resting nicely on his chest. Pinned is what he was.

"What in thunder!" he sputtered. His eyes were about ready to fall out of their sockets, but that was likely due to the fire he was seeing in my own eyes.

"Don't talk 'bout thunder 'til you seen the lightning, son, and I'm 'bout to strike." I pushed Mister Henry a tad harder against his chest, which made him go pale in the face.

"You're making a scene," he said in desperation. That's one of those fancy words back-easterners have for keeping arguments off the streets. But there wasn't much of an audience here now. Hell, I didn't care if the whole town was watching!

"What I'm gonna make is a busted head!" Growl? Son, there are wilder grizzlies that have been brought out of hibernation by accident that spoke softer than I did just then!

"Please, let's be civilized about this."

I reckon if I'd have pushed much harder, he would have turned a quick few shades of color and died on me, so I eased up and let him catch his breath. Besides, there was a bit of a crowd gathering now, and one of them was the kid I'd given my horses to a short time back. The kid, apparently, was the only one who had enough guts to speak his mind.

"Don't you go away," I said to Carston as the boy approached.

"What is it, son? Got some problems with the horses, do you?"

"No, sir, Mister Ezra," he said with a shy, standoffish look, the way kids will. "I wanted to know if I could talk to you sometime."

"Why, shore, son," I said in my best mountain-man dialect. "It'd be tetotacious pleasur'ble to. Right now, though"—I nodded toward Carston—"I got some business to take care of. You understand."

I was turning back to Carston when I heard it. Cackling. The kid had started it by calling me Mister Ezra, but, hell, you couldn't blame him, for he didn't know me from nobody. The cackling is how it usually began, and this time wasn't any different as I turned to see a few faces that I recognized from the mob that we'd stood off recently.

"Ez-z-z-z-ra?" one of them teased. My business with Robert Carston was going to have to wait.

Once you get out to this land, you learn that there are two things you can't hold against a man; one is his heritage and the other is his name; because he never had any part in choosing either of them. It's sort of an unwritten law of the land, you might say. Of course, every once in a while you run into yahoos like these that go against the grain, and it was them I'd been fighting all my life. Fists, guns, knives, take your pick. I'd started holding my own as a youngster, which is another reason I'd gotten to be as old as I was.

"Don't get pushy, mister. I'm in a bad enough mood as it is. You've had your fun, so move on. I got more intelligent people to talk to."

He didn't like that much, and neither did his friends, a group that seemed to have grown to five or so. Fact is, one of them was feeling right froggy then, making his way toward me on the boardwalk from the kid's side.

"Out of my way, kid." He said it mean like, pushing the boy aside as he kept his eyes on me. The lad careened off the wall of the building we were in front of, giving out a short cry of pain, and his hand flew to his shoulder where he'd been hit. By now it was too far gone to stop.

The ruffian who'd shoved the boy was coming at me from my left, for I was still facing the crowd before me. Mister Henry was in my right hand so I balled up that left fist and shot it out in his direction. The force of the blow landed square on his chest, stunning him if nothing else. I brought Mister Henry around in one quick motion, and I wasn't the only one who heard hard metal strike bone when the gun made contact with his elbow. He retreated only one step, but it was all that was needed because that boy had regained his balance and had placed his foot behind the man, sending him sprawling to the boardwalk. I made short work of giving the boy a quick smile and saying, "Handy, son, handy."

Always take the high ground if fighting's what you have in mind. There's something about looking down on people that tends to make them wonder how you got into that position in the first place. Sometimes it even gives them second thoughts about taking you on. One of the loud-mouths was stepping up onto the boardwalk when I brought Mister Henry back ninety degrees and whacked him alongside the noodle, which tends to make the rest of your body feel as mushy as your brain, and he, too, went a-sprawling.

Robert Carston had taken a hand in this game and was holding his own from what I could see. I never was big on miracles, but considering that he hadn't joined those ya-hoos against me after what I'd done to him, well, I reckon such things do exist. About the same time that fellow turned to mush, one of his compadres landed flat on his back beside him. All I know is that with the one quick glance I gave to my left, I saw Robert rubbing his fist in the palm of his hand. Doesn't matter how many fights you get into, I don't believe you ever get used to the pain of bone meeting bone—it just ain't natural.

"That's right, lad, you just step right up," I said to a fourth of the group who'd planted one foot on the board-walk. But he stopped in his tracks when I shoved Mister Henry into his chest. "Call, raise, or fold, son; it don't make no never mind to me, long as you keep in mind that any move but the last one is going to get you dead." I meant business and he knew it, as his foot soon took its proper place on the ground.

"How are you without the rifle?" a voice to my side said, and I turned to see the first loudmouth, the one the boy and I had taken care of, standing there bold as life. Only now he had the boy in front of him, a knife poised at the lad's throat.

The mad I had felt toward Robert couldn't match the anger that was filling my system now.

"Robert, keep an eye on these pilgrims," I said, handing the rifle over to him, all the time my gaze set on the tough before me. To the man who'd run his mouth, I said, "I'm the hoss that tain't never been rode, sonny. Fact is, on my worst day I've taken on better men than you'll ever be. What this chile's wondering is how you are toe to toe 'thout having to hide behind someone."

"You asked for it, mister," he said, a mean leer coming to his face as he released the boy.

"So did you, pilgrim." There couldn't have been more than six steps between us as I headed for him. He still had that knife in his hand, but I was about as fed up with civilized bullies as could be and didn't really care at this point. And I take big steps when I get riled.

Well, that boy was right gamey. As soon as this fellow had taken the knife away from his throat, he'd gone to the rear, presumably out of the line of fire. But when he saw me walking toward the man with no weapon but my fists, he stepped up behind that yahoo and kicked him. Hard. In the back of the calf. Now, friend, if you've ever been hit in that spot, well, you'll know that it gets your attention real quick. The ruffian grimaced and gave a fast look to his rear to see who it was that had done it. That was all I needed.

When he turned his head back, I knocked it right back to the position it had just left. He was big, this one, but like I've told my boys, big don't necessarily mean tough, and this one wasn't. I swung a left up into his gut, knock-

ing the wind out of him, and hit him in the face again.
Twice. It was the third blow that staggered him, and this
time when he fell it was without help from the lad's fancy
footwork. He wasn't unconscious yet and still had that knife
in his hand, so I made quick work of dropping one knee
onto his chest as I pulled my bowie and let him feel just
the tip of it under his scraggly beard.

"I can't brea—" he started to say.

"That's the idea, son. You know, I sure hope you like
this town, 'cause the next time I run across you I'm going
to make you a *permanent* resident. Comprende?" I didn't
have to tell him that I meant I was going to make sure he
got planted in the nearest graveyard; the fear in his eyes
said he knew all about that. "Plenty of flatland out there
that ain't been seen yet, I hear. You look like you travel
light. Was I you, I'd find me a different territory and a
different line of work. Having a big mouth never did make
a big man."

The crowd dispersed and soon there was only me, Robert, and the boy.

"You can be right handy to have around, son," I said
to the lad. "Got a name, do you?"

"Jaime." He pronounced it first the Spanish way, then
settled on the American pronunciation. His hair was dark,
his skin tinted with the olive color of those from south of
the border; a breed of sorts, most likely. His trousers and
shirt were simple but worn. Whoever it was he belonged
to, I'd a notion they'd fallen on starving times.

"Where's your home at?"

He shrugged. "Where I make it."

"Where are your parents?" Robert asked, concerned.

Another shrug. Silence.

This purely stumped Robert Carston, and I got to wondering just how educated he was.

"Why, that's preposterous! Everybody has—"

"Robert, where's the best eating place in town?" I interrupted. When he gave me the information, I looked down
at Jaime. "Three, four hours at the most, you take root on

their front steps. Palavering oughtta be done after a good meal.''

His eyes lit up like the candles on a birthday cake and he promised to be there on time before he left.

''You gave a good account of yourself, too,'' I said to Robert, taking Mister Henry from his hands. I remembered then the conversation I was about to have with this man, before the fight had started. ''We still gotta talk, amigo.'' He was silent, raising a cautious eyebrow at my suggestion. ''Saloon's down the street. I'll buy you a beer.''

That made him a bit more receptive to my demands, and I'll admit I was changing my mind some about Robert Carston. Hell, maybe I'd misjudged him. I seemed to be doing a lot of that these days.

''What do you think of Callie?'' I asked when Slim had set two beers down before us.

''Well,'' he said, pausing to take a sip of his beer, ''I must confess that I've grown quite fond of her. We did spend some time together on the trip out—''

''Yeah, I know. She told me.''

''I see.'' He was somewhere between curious and cautious now, not sure where the conversation was going or what it would lead to.

Being soft-spoken and polite have never been what you call my strong virtues, but what I said next was likely the closest I ever came to that. Yes, it was.

''She figures they made an awful mistake in what you civilized folk call the census.''

''Mistake? Census?'' This fellow couldn't read sign for spit! But I held my temper, I truly did.

''Says them head counters are way off. Claims there's only one man in the country and that's you.''

I do believe I could have shot him then and he wouldn't have known what had hit him, he was that stunned.

''But I had no idea, I—''

''Course not,'' I assured him, knowing what was going through his mind. ''Callie's too shy to set her cap for a man and go about getting him the way other females will. She's gonna wait for some man to come sweep her off her feet 'cause she figures that's the way it oughtta be.'' I finished my beer. ''And maybe she's right. But then, I don't know much about romance.'' Once upon a time, perhaps, but most of it was a faded memory now.

''This certainly puts a new light on things,'' Carston said.

''That it does. Gonna be leaving tomorrow, you know. Got to get Callie out to Aunt Sarah.'' The mention of her name gave me shivers.

''You'll excuse me, Mr. Hooker,'' he said after a long silence, draining his beer and rising, ''but I have some business to take care of.''

Then he was gone.

Time went fast that afternoon and it wasn't long before I found myself heading for the eatery Carston had named. Jaime was on the door stoop, just as I'd told him to be.

''Bring your appetite, did you?'' I asked, but the question was an unnecessary one, as the rumble of his insides announced that it had been some time since it had been well-fed.

''Are we going to eat now?'' Anxious is what he was, not that I could blame him.

''Couple of minutes and we'll have a seat, unless I miss my guess,'' I said, giving an occasional glance down the street. I was right, too, for in just a few minutes Callie showed up with Robert Carston on her arm.

''Would you believe it, Ezra; Robert asked me to dinner tonight,'' she said in an astonished way. Then, with both hands, she took my face, pulled it down to hers and kissed it. ''You were right, big brother,'' she smiled, ''everything will turn out all right.''

''Betcher . . . bottom dollar,'' I said, catching myself in time. Not even a sister gets used to all the cuss words a brother picks up in this world. ''Now, I don't know 'bout you folks, but I ain't had a bite to eat since morning fire.''

When you talk about *fancy* eating places out here, you usually mean the ones that have polished furniture and individual tables that look better than the rough-hewn community tables I was sure had become all too familiar to

Callie and Robert on their trek west. Relay stations were getting famous for them, although they'd been around for some time now. The place we entered managed to get us a fair-sized table just for four. They only *started* to make a complaint about Jaime's lack of formality before I straightened them out. Not that I was out to find a reputation, mind you, but after the ruckus I'd raised in the past couple of days . . . well, incidents like those can make you a known man right quick.

Their specialty was serving up a thick piece of steak, so that was what we had. They tried passing out a plate of greens to go with the meat, but although Callie and Robert accepted it, I told the fancified waiter he could keep it, and Jaime did the same. I recalled how it was back in the 1820's when the people in this country first started eating tomatoes. Oh, they'd been around long enough, but until that time, folks always thought they were poisonous. Besides, you get used to a way of eating up in the mountains that sticks with you. The meat on my plate and the biscuits that came with it would do me fine, thank you. My turning down those greens didn't cause the only strange look I got; I ordered an extra steak for Jaime, which drew another raised eyebrow from the waiter.

"I had breakfast this morning. He didn't," I said in my best demeaning tone, and that seemed to settle it. I never have cared for people who look down on you when they're talking to you.

"Why is it that fella reminds me of the town undertaker?" I asked no one in particular when the waiter had left.

"Disposition, perhaps," Robert replied with a smile. He had the same happy look about him that Callie did; the sort of permanent smile you get when events are going so well you just know that nothing could spoil your day. It was plain that both their attitudes had changed since I'd last seen them that afternoon.

"Well, now, Robert, you look like a fella I knew oncet that thought he'd caught his whole winter's plew on the second day of spring thaw."

Whether he understood it or not, that smile didn't waver.

"I have some news that is just as welcome, I believe," he said, looking back and forth between Callie and me for our reactions. I can hold a pretty good poker face when I want to and I did then. Callie, on the other hand, had a look of hope in her eyes, if not in the flush of her cheeks, as well.

"Yes, Robert." She even sounded happy when she spoke.

"I'll be going with you and your brother when you leave tomorrow," he said, placing a large, gentle hand on hers. By then, both of them were grinning like it was Christmas morning and I had a notion that they were each about to get what they wanted so badly, whether they would admit to it in public or not. "There are enough stores here in Independence already," he said to me. "That was the business I had to take care of this afternoon, after that fracas we got in. I'd originally intended to set up a general store here, but after giving it a good deal of thought, I've decided that Lawrence, Kansas is just as profitable a place to start. The only problem is I have three wagons of goods that I'll be taking with me. I can drive one and I'd be honored if you'd take on the second for me, Mr. Hooker. If I can find another driver on such short notice . . . or if you'd know of someone . . . ." His voice trailed off.

"Oh, I don't think that'd be no problem a'tall. Jaime here, why I'd reckon he's got close to all the time in the world to learn another profession. What do you say, boy?" I asked, but I needn't have, for his face was already lit up with excitement. " 'Sides, oncet I get Callie out to Kansas, I'll likely head for them Shinin' Mountains with the lad and give him a few lessons on being a free trapper."

"But," Robert said, suddenly hesitant, "are you sure he can—"

"Mebbe back east you give your youngsters toys and such to play with, Robert, but out here they learn how to find wood for the fire and then the meat to cook over it soon as they get the feel of an ax handle and a long gun. And you seen the way he done for us this afternoon."

I gave Robert the same hard look I'd thrown at the waiter, daring him to challenge me or my reasoning. He didn't. Fellow might have some smarts after all.

"Well . . . why not," he said, the smile returning to his face.

The food came then and we ate in silence, sort of a happy silence I reckon you'd call it. Robert and Callie were going through the motions of eating but I doubt if they tasted much of anything, the way they kept giving each other fleeting glances as lovers will. As for Jaime, he wolfed down that first piece of meat like there wasn't a tomorrow. It was the second one he slowed down on, assuring me every other bite that he'd never let me down. Me, I enjoyed that meal, I really did. Oh, the food was good, but it was the company and the good feelings that surrounded us all that I hadn't experienced in a long time. After being in as many bust-ups as I had of late, it was good to be able to make so many people happy at one time, like Saint Nicholas on Christmas Eve . . . if you know what I mean.

When the meal was done, I swallowed the rest of my coffee and pushed myself away from the table, sloshing on my hat and grabbing up Mister Henry. The waiter was nearby so I dug some silver out of my pocket, paid for the food, and gave him one last instruction.

"These two are going to need a mite more coffee." I nodded toward Callie and Robert. "Got some talking to do after all that looking, I expect." The waiter disappeared, as Callie blushed at my comment. "Jaime and me have come to the important part of the day, too," I said to them. "Got some palavering to do our own selves. Be out front."

The boy wanted to know all about the mountains and mountain men and where else I'd been, so we found ourselves some vacant chairs and talked like a couple of old friends who haven't seen one another in some time. It was pleasing for me, talking to that young boy, for although I'd known him only a few short hours, I was taking a genuine liking to him. It was getting on toward dusk when Callie burst out of the restaurant, looked wide-eyed to both sides before spotting Jaime and me, and busted out crying on the way over to us. Believe it or not, she came at a run, and how a woman can move that fast in all those skirts is something I will never know.

"Oh, Ezra!" was all she said before burying her face in my chest, and I found myself wondering how much that piece of buckskin was going to tighten up on me the next day.

Some things you come to do automatically, like grabbing up your rifle when trouble's about. Robert was only a few seconds behind Callie in coming out of the restaurant, a bewildered look on his face, and I knew he'd hurt my sister in some way and that by God I was going to kill him for it! And I would have if it hadn't been for Callie holding onto me so tight and being in my way. I would have clubbed him to death, but instead I pointed Mister Henry at him and cocked my weapon.

"Put that damn thing down!" he said, looking right down the barrel and sounding as full of gumption as Bill Barnes, and I don't mind telling you that I was surprised. So far, Robert Carston had been pretty easygoing, but the tone in his voice now wasn't unlike that of some Indian chiefs I'd come across after they'd finished talking to their medicine men about the prospects of going to war.

"No, Ezra, please," Callie was saying while I spent that split second thinking on whether to flat-out kill this man or just cripple him for life. But looking down into my sister's face only brought that much more confusion to the proceedings, for although the tears were still streaming down her face, she had about the happiest smile I'd ever seen on her. "He said he wants to marry me, Ezra, don't you see? *He loves me!*"

"Jesus, Mary, and Joseph," I said, but it was more of a sigh than anything else. "Do you know how close you came to getting Green Rivered, son?"

He didn't answer because he was suddenly preoccupied with Callie coming into his arms. She had to be holding onto him tighter than she had me, and I thought I had a rib loose inside somewhere from that bear hug! Still, congratulations were in order, so I walked up behind her and took Robert's hand, giving it a good pump as I told him what a lucky man he was.

"It wasn't hard, really. I just couldn't find the right words to tell her before," he said with a smile that had a mite of humility to it. "I guess we all need a nudge in the right direction once in a while." No need to tell me what that was all about.

"You call me Black Jack from here on out," I said, as if I was letting him in on some big privilege. "Right now you'd do well to find you a good-sized kerchief or a flower garden nearby. I hate to see water go to waste."

"What about me?" Jaime asked. I'd nearly forgotten about him. "Do I get to call you Black Jack, too?" he said as Callie and Robert sauntered off toward the hotel, Callie still overwhelmed by it all.

"Why, shore, pard! Wouldn't have it no other way!" If those two pieces of meat he'd downed had satisfied his insides, being recognized by a man in a man's world had set things straight in another area with this lad.

"Why is she crying, Black Jack?" he asked. Both of us were watching the couple as they walked away.

"Only explanation I can give you for that, son, is that she's a woman. Believe me, Jaime, if I tried answering that question, it would take the rest of this night and three more days to do it, and all it would do in the end is addle your brain." I smiled at him. "And you're too young for that."

Then I went back to storytelling.

Chapter 6

True to Robert's word, the wagons were ready to roll the next morning and so were the rest of us. I had all of them up before daybreak and over to Annie's for some fixings before we left Independence. Jaime, Robert, and I fared pretty well with our food, but I think the only thing that kept Callie awake was some of the comments she drew, her being the only female in the establishment besides Annie at the time. Not that I could blame these fellows, for that morning was the first time I'd ever really seen the full outline of my sister's body, so to speak. Robert had had the good sense to buy her a pair of Levi's for this trip and I'll tell you, son, they stuck to her like dried buckskin after a good rain!

She always did have the prettiest face in the family, but with those denims and a man's shirt, why, you could tell she was one who'd never get sick; all you had to do was look at the woman and you knew she was *healthy*, if you know what I mean. Not frail like those back-east girls, either. Out here a man looked for a woman who could bear his children, and that meant a woman who had a mite more than was needed on the hips because that's where all the pressure got put when she was in a family way. Callie, she had what was needed for bearing children and was a looker to boot.

"Better eat up, hon, this may be the last decent meal you get until Aunt Sarah's," I said as her eyes began to close again. My voice woke her, and she picked at her food some more, but she wasn't the only one who'd heard me.

"She don't need no more growing, mister," a gravelly sort of voice said from the next table. Now, friend, I don't come anywhere close to being handsome, but this fellow, why, he was downright ugly—in more ways than one by the sound of his voice. Almost reminded me of me, except for one thing. He wasn't me.

Callie can never say she didn't have people that cared about her, no sir. No sooner had Ugly said his mouthful than he had bought into a fight he definitely didn't want. Within a second I had my bowie out and was playing with that big red vein that goes up alongside the neck of the man. Robert was continuing to surprise me with his quickness, as his derringer was stuck right betwixt Ugly's eyes.

"That's my sister you're talking 'bout," I said in a hard voice.

"And my *fiancée*," Robert threw in, cocking his short gun.

"And she's a lady," I heard Jaime say behind me. He was starting to surprise me, too, for Ugly seemed to have forgotten all about my knife and Robert's short gun. When I glanced over my shoulder, I could see why. On the far side of the table, without so much as a sound, Jaime had come to a full standing position and had Mister Henry at his shoulder ready to use, pointing right at Ugly's head. Those sort of odds tend to take the air out of a blowhard's sails; tends to humble them real quick, is what it does.

"Look, I was only—"

"You made a mistake, mister," I said, likely sounding as ugly as he looked, if that was possible. "Best thing you can do is go back to shoveling food down that shaft you call a mouth afore you find out the whole mine's caving in and you're gone beaver."

That not only took care of Ugly, it brought Callie fully awake.

"Like I said, hon, eat up."

"After what happened, I—"

"Eat." I didn't ask her, I told her. Luckily she took the hint, for I lose all desire to converse when there's a plate of hot food in front of me. I've been through starving times twice, and that was twice too many to make me take eating a hot meal lightly.

"I'd like to go now," she said when she'd eaten only three quarters of the food on her plate. Not that I could blame her, mind you. Her face had turned bloodred at the beginning of the whole incident and still hadn't gone back to normal.

"Sure." I pushed myself away from the table, but felt the firm grip of Robert's hand on my sleeve.

"Jaime, why don't you take Callie out to the wagons," he said. "Black Jack and I have to finish our coffee. We'll be along shortly."

The boy eagerly did as he was told, showing traits of some sort of good upbringing, the way he helped Callie out of her chair and assisted her out through the entrance. When they had left, I looked down at my half-empty cup and gulped the remaining warm liquid.

"There, coffee's done," I said. Out the window I could see the first bright colors of daybreak and I felt the urge to be doing something. Everytime I see those colors I know the Almighty's seen fit to at least start the day over again.

"Are you sure you want Jaime along with us?" Robert asked, a slow frown coming to his forehead. "He could have killed that man this morning, and then we'd really be in a fix. He's only nine or ten. What I'm saying, Black Jack, is—"

"What you're saying is you don't trust him." I kept my voice low, but you can believe I had as much fire building in me as I had when old Ugly had made his remark about Callie, and before I was through, Robert Carston was going to know about it. "Well, if he'd killed that bastard this morning, I can't say as I'd have blamed him. Hell, you and me was getting ready to do the same thing! *Fix*, my aching . . . back!"

I would have said what was really on my mind if it weren't for Annie approaching the table and refilling our cups. We both smiled at her as if nothing was wrong, but as soon as she was gone I lit into Carston again.

"One thing you'd better get used to out here, Robert, is the people. You see, they're a bit like moss. They tend to grow on you. Some can be a pain in the ass, I'll grant you, but then you northeasterners have always been like that. Me, I'm heading west and I don't mind telling you that I've no objection a'tall to that lad growing into my right-hand man. That's my instinct." I took a huge gulp of coffee, then cocked what you'd call a cheeky eye at him, the way you do when you're just daring someone to challenge you; letting them know you'll fight at the drop of a hat if it's their wish. "He goes, Robert, and that's that. Besides, he reminds me of my boys and—" I stopped short, but I reckon Robert saw that what was on my mind wasn't something I wanted to talk about; and, like most curious folk, he wanted to know more.

"And?"

"None of your business, son. He just goes." I'd known men who'd been shot for asking just that one question; Robert was lucky I wasn't in the mood for talking or killing just then. "Now finish your coffee, we're burning daylight," I told him.

What with driving those loaded wagons and all, I figured we'd be at least a week late getting to Aunt Sarah's, but like I said, she and I weren't too fond of each other anyway. It was Callie who did all the worrying for both of us. By the end of each day she was eager to know how much progress we'd made on our trip and how much longer it would be, as if that wasn't already engraved in her memory from the day before. Well, friend, sister or not, a man's got a limit to being pestered.

"I heard a few years back 'bout a bunch of youngsters they was calling the Pony Express," I said when we made camp the third night, and Callie started asking the same questions over again. "Dee-livered the mail, they did. Rode some seventy miles a day they say, and some went more than a hundred or two at a stretch."

"I heard about them," Jaime said, his eyes lighting up again. "I wanted to ride with them, but"—here his voice lost its enthusiasm—"I wasn't old enough."

"But what does that have to do with anything, Ezra? I asked you how far we'd come today and how far we have to go before we get there." Maybe it was being anxious about getting there so late that made her get that uppity just then; maybe it was her way. Whatever it was, I wasn't having any of it!

If she couldn't see the storm clouds gathering on my face, she must have been blind or didn't care. I knew Callie's eyesight was likely better than mine, so she must not have cared. Women are like that at times, you know.

"What does the Pony Express have to do with anything!" she all but screamed in fury.

Jaime had been wisely staying out of it, breaking up firewood on a dead stump all the while. But when I picked Callie up by grabbing her under the arms and moved straight forward about six steps to Jaime's stump, the lad pushed everything off of it as quick as you please. When I planted her on that stump it was with the same force you use to bust open a piece of deadwood, I set her down that hard.

"Set and shut up." My putting her there had shocked her all right, but it was the tone of my voice that made her sit up and take notice, for I doubted she'd ever been talked to that way. Robert took a step toward me, a stern look about him, but I cocked just that one eye at him that was enough to say, butt out, and he did. Hell, he wasn't married to her *yet*!

"The last time anyone got that close to acting uppity with me that I didn't bust up was old Ezekiel hisself, and that was because he bit me in the ass and I was running hard as I could to get away from him!" Callie was about ready to lose her eyeballs, and I do believe that I could have pulled a tooth if I'd wanted to, her mouth was hanging so far open. Jaime and Robert were taking it all in. "You move your get-up-end off'n that stump, darlin', and I'm going to find something in these wagons that's hard and flat and blister your bottom so bad you'll think you was born with calluses!

"I mentioned those Pony riders 'cause they was riding light and on the back of wild mustangs with a good bit of bottom to boot! The string that's pulling these wagons is second-rate at best, and with what we're hauling, we're lucky to get fifteen miles a day out of 'em!

"Now, Sis, I don't mind telling you that Jaime here asks me questions all day long and I don't mind 'em, not one bit. But he only asks each question *oncet*. Now, if you want me to get you to Aunt Sarah, I'd ad-vise you to start making use of yourself 'round here."

"But—"

"When you see the outline of what looks like buildings on the horizon, Callie, you just lay the reins to that team of yours and hope they don't die on you from the excitement. *That* is when we will be there."

Flustered is what Callie was. She had all sorts of things to say but couldn't pick which one to start with, so she said what most females do when they get that way and their mate's about.

"Robert! Do something!"

He knew he was damned if he did and damned if he didn't. The difference was that tangling with me was going to hurt more than his pride, which was all that Callie was really suffering from now, anyway. On the other hand, even if she was wearing those denims, he had an opportunity to show her who was really going to wear the pants in the family. If he was man enough.

He was.

"You're absolutely right, my dear," he said, approaching us. That action seemed to satisfy Callie, thinking that her would-be husband was about to fine-tune me. But her satisfaction was short-lived, for Robert gave her a condescending look and said, "If I were you, I'd take your brother's advice . . . and start making some supper for us." Turning to the boy, he added, "I'll split the rest of this deadwood, Jaime, if you'll see if you can find some more."

The only time I ever saw Mama really get mad at Pa, she got so red in the face, and that vein alongside her throat got so big that I thought she was going to bust a gut then and there. The look on Callie's face was the very same now as she stood and glared back and forth from Robert to me.

"Men!" she yelled and stomped off toward one of the wagons.

I winked at Robert, sort of giving him my approval, you might say, and smiled at Callie's retreating back, remembering how beautiful she looked when she got fired up like that.

"Sis," I said, more to myself than anyone, "that ain't the half of it."

Chapter 7

I don't think Robert had ever seen a woman so relieved to reach a town she was heading for as Callie, or a man so filled with apprehension as me. It wasn't but a couple of days after my lecture to my sister that we pulled into Lawrence. To say that Callie and I had been hardheaded ever since that talking-to was putting it lightly. The food had been as bland as any of the trail meals I'd ever eaten, Robert had been cautious, and Jaime was taking it all in with a smile. Fact is, I do believe the boy was the only one enjoying himself those last couple of days of the trip.

Lawrence wasn't more than a small to medium-sized frontier town of two or three hundred people, but if you didn't know it was a hotbed in this silly war they were fighting, friend, well, you just weren't up on your news. "Bleeding Kansas" had been the stomping grounds for John Brown and his boys before the war had officially begun and it hadn't healed up any of its wounds since. Even I knew that, and I usually stayed as far away from towns as I could; nothing but trouble is what civilization is.

Harpers Ferry had taken care of John Brown, but now that it was suddenly legal to start shooting at whomever you saw in the distance just because you thought he "looked" like a northerner or southerner, a few more players had decided to sit in on the game. Guerrilla warfare had become the order of the day, and both sides had taken to enlisting men who couldn't have been more than second-rate outlaws at best, to my mind. A fellow by the name of Mosby was calling his men "Rangers" down south; McCulloch, down in Texas, had some real-life, used-to-was Rangers to fight the war with; and out here in Kansas and Missouri they had Jayhawkers and Red Legs, supposedly fighting for the North, and raiders like those led by that Quantrill character I'd been hearing about on the Southern side. It didn't matter who they were to me. It wasn't my war and I wanted no part of them or it. Hell, I'd known old mountain men who had shady pasts, who were more honest than the men out riding the range today! Cutthroats just doing for themselves is what they were.

Fact is, that was the only apprehension I had about bringing my sister to this particular town, for Lawrence was abolitionist all the way, and that made the place about as safe as Fort Sumter the day they fired on it. Now you know why I wanted the man who was going to accompany my sister to this neck of the woods to have more than a back-east education, and I was convinced that if Robert could handle that derringer of his, he'd do fine with a long gun.

"Callie, is that you?" Aunt Sarah called out when we pulled up in front of her house. Sis didn't need any ladylike helping hand to get off the wagon that time. Sarah hadn't finished speaking when Callie was down off that seat and the two were hugging one another like long lost relatives, which I reckon they were. Robert, Jaime, and me just looked on while all this took place, the two women finally holding each other at arm's length to gauge one another. I don't know why in the hell they do it that way, but they do. It wasn't hard telling that Sarah was surprised by Callie's manlike look, but she must have wanted to savor the moment. So did I.

"How did you find me? I know that Lawrence is a small town, but—"

"Wasn't hard at all," I said, speaking up for the first time and looking as dead serious as I could. "When we came to the edge of town I just asked one fella who was the ugliest woman hereabouts, and he pointed out your place.'' Jaime was holding a hand over his mouth in an unsuccessful attempt to stifle his laughter, and even Robert was having a hard time keeping a straight face.

Not that you could blame them. Sarah Hooker was short and thin to the point of looking frail, but in truth a feistier woman never lived, unless it was Callie. Her hair was tied back in a bun at the back of her head in what seemed like an unsuccessful attempt at straightening out the wrinkled prune face below it, which had been set in granite so many years ago. Plenty of women have looks a man could likely call homely, but when I looked at Aunt Sarah I saw ugly, and you've got to go some for that. And after the comment I'd just made, frail or not, she appeared ready to fight wildcats.

"Was that really necessary, Ezra?'' Callie said, giving me just as fighting a glance as Sarah's.

"Hell, yes!'' I said, letting a bit of a smile show so they'd know I was enjoying myself. "Been wanting to say it for years.''

"You . . . you, troublemaker!'' was all Sarah could muster.

"So some say.'' I glanced at Sarah, then at Callie in what you might call a mischievous way. "I had a talk with Sis on the way up here, Sarah. Set her straight on some things. Let her know that if ever she got uppity again I'd find me a *flatiron* to take to her bottom.'' That statement didn't do much to ease my sister's temper, but it took the wind right out of Sarah's huffiness quick as you could wink. "Now, have you got some place I can water and feed these teams? They came a far piece and need looking after worse than we do.'' She pointed out a big red barn. "You think you can bile up a pot of coffee, Sarah? I know you're going to want to make us feel *at home*.'' Times like this I put on my best mountain man accent, especially since Sarah was the first to ever have called me a heathen for going off to the mountains.

We had enough work tending those horses to keep us busy a good share of the rest of the afternoon. Even if they weren't the best animals I'd ever seen, they had done the job of getting us to our destination and deserved more than a cussing-at.

"*Was* that really necessary?" Robert asked after we'd been working on the teams in silence a few minutes. I could feel the back-east honorable gentleman in him coming out again.

"You bet. Comes to Sarah, I always let her know right off where it is I stand with her, case she figures I've got soft over the years."

"Why did she get so quiet?" Jaime asked with a boy's inquisitiveness.

"Jaime, that's really none of—"

"Truth is, son," I said, interrupting Robert, "flatirons tend to make her nervous, particularly 'round me. You see, some years back, when I was setting off for the mountains, old Sarah made a visit to the house just afore I left. She was young then but still ugly as a horned frog. Thing with Sarah is, she's always made up for her ugliness by being bossy. Only two people it never worked on."

"You?" the boy asked anxiously.

"Yup."

"Who else?" I had him hooked on this story like a hungry big-mouth bass. As for Robert, he was still currying his horse, but I had a feeling his ears were as wide open as the boy's.

I smiled, remembering. "Pa."

"Really?"

"You bet. That day, you see—the day I was fixing to leave—Sarah was getting tarnational pushy with Mama and Pa concerning my going. Mama, she was the patient one in the family. It was Pa that Aunt Sarah pushed too far.

"He dragged her out to the barn when he couldn't stand no more, laid her across his knee, took up the thick piece of flatiron he used to feed the fire near his anvil with, and put 'bout as many calluses on Sarah as I promised to give Callie." I smiled again, remembering the incident. "I do believe that was the day Aunt Sarah took a genuine hatred to the men in the world."

Robert smiled, although I couldn't be sure he believed

that tall tale or not. Jaime's reaction was a mixture of awe and laughter.

By the time we got close to finishing, the wind had shifted a bit, and it was evident that the women had taken to cooking the evening meal. Callie had silently brought out two cups of coffee for Robert and me and water for the boy after we'd been at those horses a half an hour. But that had been the only time we'd seen her, and smelling whatever it was they were cooking only made us wash up that much quicker.

It wasn't Sunday that I could tell, but Callie and Sarah sure had the table laid out like it was. About half the size of a relay station table, it had settings for five with as fancy a tablecloth as you'd ever see in a restaurant; and on it were a ham and a few side plates of beef, all steaming and hot, with homemade biscuits, all of which I'd had a taste of before.

"You know, Sarah, I always did say you could cook." I made sure to take that beaver pelt off my topknot and find a corner to set Mister Henry in rather than leaning him up against the table like I was used to. On good behavior is what I reckon you'd say I was as we all took our seats.

"Yes, and you always said it just before you sat down to one of my meals." Now, she was speaking the truth, friend, I'll not deny it one bit. It's just the *way* she was speaking it that I never did care for—uppity like if you will. But what the hell, I figured; I was about to eat a meal that I hadn't cooked, and if you've been on the trail long as I have, why, those are the best by far. Yes, sir.

I was about to cut off a chunk of meat when Sarah gave me a hard look that said if I didn't stop immediately I wouldn't be eating at her table for long.

"You did put this here to eat, didn't you?" Now, maybe that was a stupid question to ask, but you'd have asked the same one if you were as hungry as I was. " 'Cause I'll tell you, Sarah, if you expect me just to sit here and admire it, I'll likely die of starvation afore the day's out."

"In *my* house we say grace before meals, Ezra." She had to be the only woman I ever knew who could act like she had starch in her neck and couldn't stare but straight ahead when she took the notion to. Stubborn. But like I said, this was food we were dealing with.

"Then by all means, get on with it," I said, being as pleasing as I could.

"I think that now that we have a man at the table, he should lead us in prayer." She had a sly look about her now, and I knew she was out to get me, meal or no meal.

"You heard her, Robert," I said, then glanced back at Sarah whose expression hadn't changed one bit. "Right eddicated, this lad," I said to her. "Likely got some real fancy prayers he can throw at you."

"No," she said slowly, dragging it out as she took on the look of a cat who's got a mouse up against the wall. "I think I'd like to hear *you* say grace, Ezra."

"Well, now," I said, not sure if there was a frog in my throat or I was going hoarse or I was just plain scared—a bit of all three I suspect. "I don't recall being in this kind of spot afore. You got something special in mind, Sarah, something in particular you want to hear?"

"Yes, I'd like to hear how it is you heathens give thanks for your daily bread." That was it, she was going to try to make a fool out of me in a territory I wasn't familiar with at all.

"I see," I said, feeling pretty humble because she was probably going to succeed. Something struck me then; maybe it was the way the boy looked at me, like he was about to lose faith in me, that did it. All I know is that of a sudden I got real determined to set Aunt Sarah straight on us "heathens."

"Well, now," I said, folding my hands together more in a clasp than with any of that fancy fingering the missionaries will give you, "seems to me Mama used to say something to the effect of blessing the food and the people at the table and thanking the Lord for it." I gave a quick glance to the roof. "So you do that, Lord, to these people and this here food, and I thank you." Then I turned to Sarah with a scowl that was intended to put her slyness to rest for some time.

"As for me and my mountains, Sarah, let me tell you when I wake up in the morning up there, I know it was my Maker had to have a hand in country as beautiful as that. I see the sun go down at the end of that day and I thank Him for bringing me through it. I doubt many of us mountain men ever went to anything close to your church services, but that don't mean we don't know who our Maker is or when it's time to tally up what we owe and make our peace with Him. You see, Sarah, in that respect I ain't no more a heathen than you are.

"Now, if you want to dissect my past and go over it one trail at a time, you do just that," I concluded, pulling out my bowie knife, an act which put the fear back in Sarah's eyes. "Me, I'm gonna dissect this ham here and eat it afore it gets any colder."

That didn't make things any easier between Aunt Sarah and me, but we did manage to get through supper in what they term a civilized fashion. The only other point that almost got touchy was having to explain Jaime.

"I didn't realize you had a son, Mr. Carston," Sarah said when we were nearing the end of the meal, giving the boy a look-over.

"Son?" At first it puzzled Robert. "Oh, no, no, ma'am. I've never been married before." That let him off the hook.

"But, he's not . . ." She let it trail off unanswered as she looked to Callie in anticipation.

"No, I never—" Callie was sounding as confused as everyone else, and I wasn't too keen on the turn this trail was taking my own self.

"Jaime's my partner," I said, as if it were nothing. That didn't do anything for Sarah's desire for an explanation, but it sure did round the day off like it was Christmas for that boy, the way his face lit up.

"But he's only—"

"He's right handy to have around is what he is, Sarah. Handled them reins like he'd been doing it near all his life on the way out here. Saved my hide a time or two back there in Independence, too. If a body can do that, he can ride with me anytime." I squinted and smiled when I continued, just so Sarah'd know it was a smart-ass remark meant especially for her. "That's how us heathens do it in the mountains." I pushed myself away from the table, sort of excusing myself whether they liked it or not, you might say. "Fine fixins, Sarah," I said, belching. "Robert, why'n't you tell Sarah 'bout Jaime and Independence. Me and the boy got some palavering to do."

"Gee, you sure do surprise people a lot, Black Jack," Jaime said when I'd refilled my coffee cup and we'd taken a seat on Sarah's porch.

"Course!" I replied in true mountain-man fashion. "How do you think I stayed alive this long?" The boy was quick, I'd seen that right off, and he was picking up on damn near everything I uttered to him, storing it away for future use.

We must have sat there for a good hour, me storytelling and him listening, while every once in a while we'd hear the high pitch of Sarah's voice as she asked Robert another question. I felt good talking to that boy, for what I'd told Robert back in Independence was true for the most part. Jaime asked the same questions Matthew and Jedediah, my boys, did when they were his age, only more of them. And Daniel . . . there would always be Danny. But I pushed him from my mind and concentrated on the lad beside me now, thinking maybe I could add something to his life. He had that kind of effect on me, Jaime. Why, I was even forgetting about Aunt Sarah.

"How old are you, Black Jack?" the boy asked, likely wanting to figure if he'd ever live to that ripe an old age.

I smiled. "Near as I can figure, my body's been 'round fifty, maybe more years. Important thing to keep in mind is that age ain't nothing but how old you feel in your mind. How old am I? Shoot, boy, I'm as old as the itch. Why, I remember when—"

"I heard that! Every word of it!! How dare you speak of me that way!!"

I didn't have to turn around to know it was Sarah, but I turned just the same, for I'd had my fill of her today. Standing there I towered over her, and the boy got up next to me. There was Sarah, mean as ever, looking to cause trouble like she always had.

"What in tarnation are you talking about?" I asked, feeling the fire build in me, knowing it would come to no good.

"I heard what you said about me!" she said in that high squeaky voice she used when she was mad. And she was drawing a crowd, which is likely what she wanted, too, as Robert and Callie soon appeared behind her.

"You? I ain't been talking 'bout you a'tall." I hadn't grasped what it was she was complaining about, but the boy had. Like I say, he was quick on the uptake.

"You're mistaken, ma'am," Jaime said with every bit of manners you could want. "Black Jack said *itch*, not—"

She slapped him. Hard. The shock that registered on his face was evident but only temporary, as his eyes widened and an urge to fight came into them. In that split second I could read more hurt in those eyes than he'd ever admit to, and I understood every bit of it. This boy was going to be a fighter and he wasn't going to take any more abuse; *not ever* is what those eyes were saying. I put a hand on his shoulder to steady him, as well as to keep him from tearing Sarah apart then and there.

"Got that outta your system, did you?" My voice drops some when I get riled, and friend, riled doesn't come anywhere close to how I was feeling then!

"No!" Sarah brought out the hatefulness in her again by slapping me across the face, too! Now, having a growth of hair on your face tends to soften the shock when someone takes an open hand to you, but being hit has never been something I've ever gotten used to, and I'd be lying if I said I wasn't feeling the same urge as Jaime then.

"Now, you listen to me, you envious, ugly old *bitch*," I said, drawing the last out so she'd know the meanness I was capable of, too. "You do that again and I'll slap *you* silly." If I was a rattlesnake, you can bet I'd have been spitting venom at her. To the boy I said, "To say they frown upon the hitting of women out here is putting it lightly, son, but you mind what I'm a-saying. This one here, she ever does that to you again, you slap her right back. Can't but help her disposition.''

''How dare you!''

''Dare?'' I shot back at her. I poked a finger at her, backing her up against the wall so she had no way of escaping. ''You call *me* a troublemaker and then go making all the trouble! Dare?''

''Ezra, maybe she—'' Callie interrupted from inside.

I was about to tell Robert he'd better get a hold of that woman of his, when I heard him say, ''Shut up, Callie, this is none of your business.''

Callie was a lot wiser than Sarah.

''But you . . . you called me ugly!'' It was a word Sarah never had gotten used to, for all the wrong reasons.

''Damn right! And I meant it,'' I said. She was starting to cry some now, but like it or not she was going to hear me out. ''Ugly? Hell, woman, I've seen men and women so ugly-looking that seeing them was like walking through that forest I seen oncet and gawking at those pee-trified trees! Didn't make no never mind though, 'cause I worked with 'em fine. By looks, Sarah, I'd say you're 'bout the homeliest woman I ever did see. The ugly's what's inside of you, and that I purely hate.''

I stepped down off the porch, then stopped to look back at the woman who was truly in tears now.

''You set a fine table, Sarah, but as for hospitality . . . well, I'd feel more at home in the middle of a Blackfoot war party. I'll be leaving tomorrow.''

''Me, too,'' Jaime said.

Sometimes you have to be by yourself to sort things out. I reckon Jaime knew that as well as me, for he drifted off on his own for a while and let me do the same. I wonder sometimes if being hurt by words isn't worse than some of the bullet and arrow wounds I've been through. You pull the lead or shaft out of them and the wound heals and you get on with your life, hoping it won't happen again. When it does, it's the same process all over again. Oh, you learn from it, all right; you have to or you'd be dead the next time someone tried driving a knife in you all the way up to the Green River. But words are another matter. The scars words leave are the inside kind, and maybe it's having too many of those that builds up the ugly in you. Maybe it was too many years of being called ugly that had made Aunt Sarah that way. I don't know. What did cross my mind watching that sun set out there was that for as tough an old bird as Sarah made herself out to be . . . well, maybe she wasn't all that tough after all.

I was coming back toward the house, walking alongside the big red barn, when I heard the crying. It was the soft kind, the kind a woman will do into her kerchief when she's grieving alone. Sobbing, I reckon you'd call it. At first I thought it might be Callie crying over what Robert had said to her earlier, but a few more silent footsteps proved it to be Sarah. Well, let her cry, I thought, and was about to head back to the barn when I heard Robert's voice.

"Life is hard, isn't it?" he said. I hadn't seen him walk out the door and take a seat beside her. He could have come from thin air for all I knew. Me, I just stood stock-still in the shadows. Not that I had a great interest in the conversation, mind you. I just . . . well, who wants to interrupt two people talking? You know I never do that.

"Yes," I heard Sarah sniffle. "Especially when no one likes you." More sniffling.

"Are you sure, Sarah? Really sure?" She didn't answer, and after a short silence he continued. "Black Jack can be quite rude, you know. Always interrupting people, sometimes forcing his own beliefs on others rather than giving them a choice in the matter. Oh, he has a number of faults. But I didn't stop there when I first met him; I didn't give up on him just because he can be abrasive." Even in the dark, I could feel the red crawling up my back.

"We've been through a couple of scrapes together, and I've come to know that if he believes in you, he'll stand by you. And I think that young boy will turn out a lot like Black Jack."

No reaction. Just silence, although the crying had stopped.

"You know, one thing I like about Callie is that she's constantly looking for the good in a situation." He had guts, Robert did, for what he did next was play his hole card against what could have been a stacked deck. Particularly since he and Sarah were going to be in the same town with one another. "Perhaps if you tried finding some good in people, Sarah, you wouldn't get so much ridicule yourself."

There was more silence and then an audible sigh, although I couldn't hear if anything was being said. I couldn't believe what I wasn't hearing, if you know what I mean. Old Robert must have pulled it off. The next sound I heard was of him getting up, followed by the voice of Sarah Hooker in what had to be the friendliest tone she had ever used in her entire life.

"I think I'm going to like you, Robert."

There was no reply, but she did stir around enough to let me slip out of the shadows, the conversation being over and all.

As I came to the front porch I heard Callie humming a tune from it. There wasn't any sun to look at, for it had already set. Maybe it was the moon coming out that did it for her. All I know is she was real content with the way the world was right then.

"Oh, Ezra, you startled me," she said when I walked up behind her.

"Sorry. Didn't mean to." While she was facing me, I leaned over and kissed her forehead, which sort of surprised her I think. "You got a real bargain in Robert, Callie. A real good man. You hang on to him."

She looked at me in a curious sort of way, as I slipped back into the night again.

At daybreak the next morning, Jaime and I were ready to leave when Robert appeared in the barn.

"There's food waiting for you in the house, you know," he said. Tell me about it, son, I thought. I'd gotten a good whiff of it half an hour ago and so had the boy, judging from the way that empty pit he called a stomach was growling, but neither of us had commented on it.

"Can't be burning daylight, Robert. Them Shinin' old Mountains is a ways from here and me and Jaime got us a trail to make."

"Well, what about my supplies?" he asked, trying another tactic. "It'll take me close to a month to get set up if I only have myself to do the unloading." It was the boy's sympathy he was trying for now, knowing that Jaime wanted to please as much as he could, but I wasn't having any of it.

"Robert, let me tell you something," I said in what likely wasn't the friendliest voice I'd ever spoken in, "I'd rather crawl into a nest of rattlesnakes—feet first, to boot!—than be seen with that woman, much less stay with her!" I checked the cinch and gathered up the reins of my mount. "No, thank you, sir. I been treated better by varmints that knew I was just passing through. That one in there has *always* figured me for a danger to her. Don't ask me why, but she has."

"She won't be a problem," he said in a pleading voice. "I promise she won't." Then, in a different tone; one that didn't sound like he was trying to compete with Crockett to see if he could talk the birds out of the trees, he said, "Besides, I don't have a best man. And Callie should have someone who's not a stranger to her to give her away."

"Now, don't go relative on me, Robert." If I sounded defensive, it was because I felt that way. To Jaime I commented, "They do this to you all the time. Everything else fails, they talk to you 'bout what you owe your relatives." I knew that the best-man angle had been thrown out to Jaime, and the boy took it, hook, line, and sinker. It was me Robert wanted to give Callie away at their wedding, something that had never crossed my mind until now.

"She really wants you to be here for the wedding, Black Jack," he said and I knew he meant it; knew Callie wanted it that way, too. Or maybe that's the excuse I used for giving in just this one time. After all, no one tells Black Jack Hooker what to do. No one.

"All right, but for one week only, understand?" I said.

"Understood." He was smiling as he gratefully pumped my hand, and the boy all but dragged us toward the house as fast as he could. Halfway across the yard, Robert smiled again. "Of course, it might take two weeks."

Without losing a step, I gave him a sidelong glance that was pure squint and dare, as I said, "Son, don't push your luck."

Chapter 8

That one week stretched into two, for all the civilized reasons townfolk will give. Callie and Sarah, of course, had to have enough time to make the wedding dress, or so they said. The wagons could have been unloaded in one day, if a body was in a hurry, but Robert was taking his own sweet time about finding the right location and just the right amount of space to rent out for the store he had in mind. Or so he said. Me, I suspicioned this whole maneuver was being put on to try to civilize me and the boy, the way your enemy will pull a flanking movement on you just when you've got your pants down. This so-called civilization, well, hoss, it scared me something fierce. But how could I explain to these people that after living in the wilds as long as I had, I'd learned that it's the humans rather than the griz and diamondback that are the most dangerous animals. They'd never have believed it, not these *civilized* folk.

The biggest surprise in those two weeks was that Aunt Sarah got as hospitable as could be toward me and the boy. Her complaining was minimal and she stopped acting like she was the free trapper and I was the beaver and to hell with how she caught me. She even smiled. Had to be a strain on her those first few days, but soon I got to wondering if maybe Robert's words hadn't sunk in after all.

I would have left halfway into that second week—I was getting that restless—if it hadn't been for the house. Robert was one of those fellows who made friends quickly and knew how to hang onto them. In that first week, while locating his new store, he had made a goodly number of acquaintances among the next-door businesses and the townfolk. I reckon you could say he had a way about him, but most businessmen are like that.

"Don't know how much longer I can take this, Robert," I said about midweek. "Getting too peaceful 'round here. Got the feeling I oughtta be moving on."

"It's only three more days until the wedding." He smiled. "Besides, we're going to build a house on Friday."

"A house building?" He had me a mite confused.

"Yes. I'm really quite grateful, actually." He paused a moment in thought. "How can I describe it? Everybody pitches in. It's sort of a work party and a town gathering, all in one. It's a . . . it's a . . . rendezvous, yes, that's what it is!" I could see the boy in him coming out; he had the same look Jaime often did, full of pride and excitement all rolled into one.

"Rendezvous?" I said in disbelief. "Come on, son, don't josh an old-timer like that. Why, there ain't been a rendezvous since back in '40."

"Well, this is probably the closest you'll ever come to one anymore. I think you'll like it."

He was right. I did.

Civilization was not only running the Indians off of their own land, it was making game scarcer. We had to go south a ways to find them, but the buffalo herds had come north to Kansas, and Jaime and I made a day of tracking down a stray that had wandered further north than he should have. Buffalo hunters could still find massive herds in the Panhandle area and Indian Territory in those years, as well as in the West, but one was all I figured we'd be needing for a handful of men putting a house together. As it turned out, what I didn't supply, the women in town did.

This house raising wasn't anything like any rendezvous I'd ever been to, but it was the next best thing, I reckon.

Children ran about like so many papooses playing games; the women set up long community tables with checkered tablecloths, on which were laid a multitude of side dishes for any and all to enjoy with their meals; and the younger men showed us how it was done, while us old bastards sat back and told stories about how we'd been roped into the very same type of activity in our youth. It was fun with a purpose in mind, which made it all that much more enjoyable.

Fact is, I had a bit of a surprise that day, too.

He came riding up in front of the half-built structure about mid-afternoon. The house being built was right next-door to Sarah's, so it wasn't out of the way, but just like those men hammering it together, I had a feeling he, too, had a purpose about him. The horse had the same lazy motion riding up as I knew the man in the saddle had about him, unless there was something urgent to be done. He wore the same flop hat as before, and the same two Colts were stuck in his waistband like I knew they'd be.

It was Bill Barnes.

Not that I was surprised to see him, mind you, for anyone could ride into town. No, it was what happened just then.

"I see you found steady work, Black Jack," Bill said with a smile, taking in the surrounding activities. "You going to settle down, too, once they got this house-raising finished?"

"Not hardly." I said it in my best mean-old-cuss voice just to let him know that he might be joshing but I wasn't. They'd plant me at the foot of some mountain before I was ever caught dead in one of these civilized places! Or hadn't you noticed?

I reckon Bill was sort of like Robert in one way. Robert, he could get a person's attention real easy, as outgoing as he was. Bill, well, he could get a person's attention, too—it's just that when he did, it was only because he wanted that person to notice him. Otherwise, he pretty much stayed in the background, from what I'd seen. But Jaime was as much in awe of Bill sitting there in his saddle like a two-gun man on the prod as he was of me and my mountain-man image, and in no time the boy was right at my side.

That's when it happened.

"Jim." I recognized Sarah's voice from behind me.

"Yes, ma'am." Nothing out of the ordinary about that, right? Of course not. Jaime was south-of-the-border for James, and Sarah had taken a notion to calling the boy Jim, although I still called him Jaime. So his replying "Yes, ma'am" as he turned to face Sarah wasn't unusual at all. It was hearing Bill Barnes atop his saddle say the same words at the same time that threw me. A quick glance at Sarah showed her to be about as surprised as I was.

"My mistake, ma'am," Bill said, grabbing the wide rim of his hat and sweeping it off in a romantic gesture like in those books where you read about the knights of old. It downright flattered Sarah, as she had never been before.

"No mistake at all, sir," she said with that awkward smile I had yet to get used to. "I was just bringing Jim a glass of punch. There's plenty, if you'd like some, and you're certainly welcome."

"I'll be back presently, ma'am. Have to take care of my horse first. If you could point in the direction of the livery, I'd be obliged."

"Oh, there's no need for that," Sarah said in what was likely the most gracious manner she'd ever shown. She'd been charmed, all right. "Why, you can use—"

"Barn's this big red one 'round the corner, Bill," I said as he dismounted. "Let me show you where it is." Not that he needed showing, you understand. Hell, if you couldn't see that barn, big and red as it was, why, you had to be either blind or dumb, and this boy wasn't neither.

It was good to see him. Outsiders were always welcome in camp if they had word of what was going on elsewhere in the States or the territory. Like it or not, Bill had given me the impression he was a lot more active than he let on, and the way he'd ridden up, as bold as you please, had to be more than just showing off for lads like Jaime. Bill wanted to make his presence known and it wasn't just to charm the ladies. Of that I was sure.

"Tracking me down, was you?" I asked when he'd finished with his horse.

He shrugged and smiled briefly.

"No, just tracking." Closemouthed wasn't the word to describe this boy. Getting information out of him was akin to panning for gold and silver out in the Colorado Territory, and you wouldn't hit pay dirt unless he wanted you to.

"You answer to Jim, too?" I asked as we started back toward the house raising. That ruffled his feathers some.

"Like I told the lady, it was an honest mistake," he replied in an even voice. Then, with a bit more hardness, he added, "You keep pushing it, Hooker, and I'm liable to go back to calling you an old man."

"Do tell," I said, cocking an eye at him. "Now, that would be real interesting."

The house raising was going too well to be interrupted by a personal dispute, so we set it aside as Bill joined the crowd and did a bit of storytelling for Jaime and the other youngsters, keeping them occupied while the women set out the fixings for what would soon be the evening meal, as the house was nearing completion right on schedule.

Now, son, you've never known what the true spirit of this frontier is until you've been to a house raising. Once it's decided just how big the house will be, you and the rest of the men get together with the sutler and gather up whatever wood, glass, nails, and tools are needed for this shindig; and whatever the sutler can't or won't contribute, you find on your own. The whole operation takes a full day most times, but you never seem to mind, even when you may not know the man you're working next to. Don't worry; by the time the day's out, you'll know him and he'll know you. Setting a foundation and nailing those walls together and standing shoulder to shoulder with another member of the community when you raise them upright . . . now, that makes for a feeling of accomplishment you won't often find other places. It comes from people working together for one another's benefit, and knowing that nobody has to make it in this land alone. That's what a house raising is. Hell, that's what this *land* is!

"He's almost as good as you are at telling stories, Black Jack," Jaime said when the food was served. "Did you know he was a spy for the Union Army?"

"Sure didn't." Lordy, could he tell tales, this Bill! It was competition like this that cooled me off a bit toward him.

"Now he's tracking down horse thieves!" the boy added between mouthfuls of food. "And I helped him out! He said so!"

"That so? Pardon me if I don't get excited all at once. You have at this buffler tongue yet? Right tasty, it is." Jaime was beginning to look like he was plum tired of being ignored, which, in all honesty, is what I was doing to him. Well, not to the boy so much as Bill Barnes. Here he was filling this boy's head with fool notions about tracking down horse thieves. . . .

"Something wrong, Black Jack?" I must have looked like the jackass that finally gave his attention to his owner after the man hit him between the eyes with a tree stump. Yes, sir, I was perking my ears right up now, and at the same time I was picking my brain for the words Jaime had just spoken so proudly.

"Where'd you say young William was telling these tall tales?" Jaime was more than helpful in locating our latest storyteller, who was shoveling food down his own gullet, all by himself, in the shade of the red barn.

"Buffalo's pretty good, Black Jack," were the first words out of his mouth as Jaime and I approached. Nodding at the boy, he said, "Told me where you got him."

If there was one thing that boy was getting good at of late, it was beaming with pride. But then, when you're a youngster his age and you manage to get most things done right, why, I reckon you can get away with looking lit up. One other lesson Jaime had picked up since we'd met was knowing when to sit back and listen, for that's as good a way of learning as reading, and he was doing that now.

" 'Pears he told you more'n that," I hinted, just in case he wanted to lead off this debate we were going to have.

"Could be," he shrugged. "I'll know more in a day or two."

"Then it's horse thieves you're tracking, like the boy says."

Bill let out a sigh the way a tired man will, either when his body's ready to give out or he's sick of playing mind games.

"Yes, I'm trailing some men who may have stolen some stock from the army. But don't go talking about it, fellas, all right? I'm playing a lone hand here, and the less anyone else knows about it, the better off I am. *Sabe?*" That last was thrown at Jaime, who immediately nodded in the affirmative.

"Son, what do you say to a refill of these here cups?" I asked the boy, handing him my tin cup, as Bill did.

"Yes, sir." Then he was gone.

"Sure you can handle six all by your lonesome?" I asked when the boy was out of earshot.

"As I recall, I did better than fair the last time I got in a scrape and you were around." He wasn't bragging, just stating a fact.

"*We*, son, we done better than fair that time," I said, correcting him.

"You really aren't gonna settle down, are you?" he said with a half-amused smile.

"Got the itch something fierce, William. This civilization is 'bout to drive me to being an old man and that ain't good, not a'tall."

Jaime was walking fast toward us, trying not to spill the two coffee cups he held.

"I reckon I can use a saddle pard for a day or two," Bill said. "Besides, that long gun of yours might just come in handy."

"Done," I said as the boy handed us our cups.

I knew there was no amount of explaining that was going to justify telling Jaime he couldn't come with me and Bill, so I waited until the day after the wedding, when Bill and I had had an early breakfast and were saddling up. The wedding had gone off just as planned, and everyone had a fine time of it; fact is, even Sarah and I'd kept from going at each other's throats that day. But that morning, as it turned out, I had more to contend with than just Jaime.

"And where do you think you're going?" Sarah asked as we brought the horses around to the front.

"We have some business to take care of, Miss Sarah," Bill said in his most flattering way. "Ought not to be gone but a day or two."

"But it's the Sabbath," Sarah protested, not taken in by him this time.

"Oh." Bill Barnes had flat lost the wind from his sails.

"Civilization," I said to him. "See what I mean?"

"Well, I can see Ezra going off like this," she continued in a huff, "but you, Mr. Barnes, why, I thought you to be a better person than that."

"Believe me, ma'am, it ain't that I'm shirking my duty," he said, trying his best not to hurt her feelings, "but I've got business that just ain't going to wait any longer."

"But how can you do that!" she said, getting louder as she went on. "You know what the Good Book says, the Lord spent six days creating this earth and—"

I knew what the rest of it was, but damn it we were burning daylight and relative or not, I reckon I just didn't have the kindness in me that Bill Barnes did.

"And on the seventh day he created women and the world ain't been the same since!" I cut in. As purple as Sarah was getting, you'd have thought what I said was blasphemy to the highest degree, or however it is you rank such things.

"Amen to that, brother." At first I thought it was Bill, but the voice had come from further away and I saw that it was Robert standing on the porch of his new house. Callie was next to him, both of them dressed in robes of a sort, and she was blushing while he had a wide grin on his face.

"Well, now, you're looking right healthy, Robert," I

said, grinning back at him. "You, too, Callie, you, too."
It brought even more blush to her cheeks when she heard
me. "I see married life agrees with you two." I just love
getting people into trouble, especially on unspeakable sub-
jects.

"Where are you going?" The newest entry into our de-
bating society was Jaime, who now appeared from around
the corner of the barn. He wasn't wearing a shirt, and I
took notice of how fast the boy was growing.

"Lad's filling out, Robert. Going to have to find him
harder work to do 'round here." When I'd gotten some
extra ammunition for Mister Henry from Robert, I'd let
him know what Bill and I were planning, so I was hoping
he'd catch on now.

"You know, you're right, Black Jack." He was eyeing
the boy in what could have been playacting if the words
hadn't sounded so sincere. "When we first ran into him,
he wasn't much more than skin and bones. You're right,
he's filling out."

"Where are you going?" Persistent cuss, this boy.

"Me and Bill got us a mite of business needs getting
took care of. Won't be gone long, son; couple of days at
the most." If you've ever gotten that uneasy feeling in the
pit of your stomach when you're trying to pass off a lie to
someone you know doesn't believe you . . . well, friend,
then you know how edgy I was feeling about then.

"You're not leaving him here, are you?" It was Sarah
again, distressed.

"Woman, I don't know why it is that you wake up every
morning with one foot in hell and the other one on fire,
but I'm fed up with it! Leave him here? Leave him here?
You think I'm gonna leave him for anything more'n a few
days with the likes of you?"

Sarah was turning blue again.

"All right, just hold on!" Robert was taking command
of the situation; at least as long as he didn't start pushing
me, he was. "Now, look, this is no way to begin a day.
Sarah, Black Jack has a point. Jaime is a good shot, whether
you like it or not, and he can provide meat for us while

these two are gone. And I don't think the Almighty is going to miss them if their seat in the pew isn't filled today. Worse things have happened."

"Miss Sarah, I'll tell you what," Bill said, being his pleasing best again. "Next time I stop by I'll make sure it's a Sunday and I'll personally escort you to the service."

"Well . . ." Sarah was giving in.

"Sarah, you feed this lad twice a day, and I'll guarantee you he'll furnish the meat for the next three meals. He's got more manners than I'll ever have, so maybe he'll do you some good." To the boy I said, "That Hawken on her mantel is still a fine piece. One shot's all you got, but you're getting good enough so's it's all you'll need. Now, I'm counting on you to take care of Aunt Sarah and give Robert whatever help he's a-needing. You've got plenty of time for adventure in your life."

With a downcast face he muttered, "Yes, sir" in a barely audible voice.

"Jim." It happened again as both Jaime and Bill looked at me. "Ain't Bill nor me running out on you. We'll be back, son. You can count on it."

Chapter 9

I must be getting feeble in my old age. Bill Barnes hadn't been stretching the blanket when he told Jaime that the boy had helped him out considerably in tracking down these horse thieves. From what he told me, Jaime had spotted some men and possibly animals on the horizon while I was skinning and carving up that buffalo we'd shot the day before the house raising. I'd gotten so consumed in preparing that animal that my senses hadn't been paying attention when they should have been. Of course, it never would have happened in the mountains, but that's something else this civilization does to you.

"Why didn't you just light a fire under your mount and take off after those fellas when Jaime gave you the information on them?" I asked at the end of the first day.

He gave me what was getting to be his usual shrug.

"Can't go far with a herd of horses without watering and feeding them every so often." Maybe that's an acceptable answer to you, friend, and maybe some greenhorn would swallow it, but I've gotten into the habit of knowing what my riding partner's up to—it's another one of those reasons I've stayed alive this long.

"Why is it I feel like a dentist whenever I'm palavering with you?" I asked in pure frustration.

"Huh?"

"Holding a conversation with you is like pulling eye-teeth!"

I'd met men like him before. They didn't do a lot of talking but you can be sure it wasn't for lack of knowing the words. They made a cat-and-mouse game of it, telling as little about themselves as they could while finding out as much about you as possible. Not that it was all that uncommon a trait on the frontier, mind you, but those who were so tight-lipped you couldn't get a name from them much less the news from the next county, well, to my mind they were either running from something or had what they thought to be the secret location of the one and only gold mine in the whole world and weren't giving it out at all. I just wasn't sure which category Bill fit into.

"You can be awful pushy, Hooker, do you know that?" he said, laying out his bedroll as the fire died down. He looked at me across those smoldering embers, and I could see fire building in his own blue eyes. "All right, mister, you want to know? Fine, I'll tell you. But you listen to me. Once I'm through talking, you can figure you've bought into this hand for good."

"Fair enough." I only gave a hint of a smile. "Long as you don't tell me these are 'dangerous men' and expect me to get skittish over it, 'cause I been dealing with them all my life."

"I've got an idea I know where they're heading and I think I know who one of them is. Town we're going to is just his type of place. He'll go there to meet someone associated with Quantrill, who's looking for horses to buy, and he'll hang around until the buyer shows up. Are you satisfied now, Hooker?"

"No dangerous men, eh?" I said half in jest, but Bill Barnes didn't have much of a sense of humor that night.

"Back shooters don't have to be dangerous, Hooker." He said it with the same dead seriousness that he had said everything else, and I don't mind telling you it made me just a tad nervous.

"Do tell."

I don't know if he was waiting for me to think it over quietly and then beg to leave before I got hurt or if he just figured that was the end of it, but the silence that lasted for a few minutes afterward had about as much tension to it as a mountain lion's hind legs before it springs into an attack. In the meantime, he propped his saddle up in place and leaned back against it.

"Hooker, I don't know how the rest of the world lets you get away with being as pushy as you are, but there's something you ought to know," he said in an even tone.

"Gitting right informative now, ain't you?"

He obviously didn't like my remark, his pale blue eyes turning cold as the Missouri River in January.

"You keep nosing around about me and what I do and you're likely to find something you ain't particularly fond of. Might turn out to be downright *painful* . . . if you get my drift."

With that he pulled that big flop hat down over his face and folded his arms across his chest, each hand resting on the butt of a pistol.

I reckon you could say *that* was the end of the evening's conversation.

You could have fooled me about that town he'd been jabbering about. It was a day and a half later that we rode into it, but it wasn't nearly as rowdy as he had indicated it would be. Looked as peaceful as a graveyard to me. We'd barely been speaking for nearly two days now, but that didn't stop Bill from taking the lead in this whole affair. After all, it was his party; I'd just been invited. We rode in the same way I'd seen him ride up to Robert and Callie's new house, slow and easy, sort of taking in the population as they did the same to us.

"You get a chill running up and down your spine riding into this place?" I asked. It was just what I was feeling then and I was glad I'd readied Mister Henry before we'd entered the town.

"Every time."

"Known in these parts, are you?"

A shrug. "Some say." But his eyes never left the streets and I had a suspicion he was thinking the same thing as I was.

Towns, even small ones, claim to be civilized, so when you ride in you usually see kids running about and women walking the streets doing the shopping just as you'd expect. So far I'd spotted three saloons and a few men walking about, but no women or kids. That meant one of two things: either this town was under someone's thumb and he knew trouble was about and had the women and youngsters hidden away, or this town wasn't anywhere close to being civilized. When I didn't see a lawman's office or anything resembling a church in the area, I tended to believe it was the latter.

"Didn't tell me I was riding into a den of thieves," I said under my breath.

"Told you it was the kind of town this fella we're tracking would head for."

We pulled up in front of one of the many saloons, every move being made in a slow manner. It wasn't so much that my bones were getting old and rickety as much as caution that made me move that way.

The saloon was dark and dank inside, my only hope being that the whiskey had as dark a color to it. If it wasn't for a plug of tobacco, I do believe most home brew would be see-through clear like Taos Lightning. My eyes were adjusting to the dark as the barkeep set up glasses in front of us and poured what the house was serving, which could have been poison for all I knew.

Not quite.

"Tolerable," I said after taking a hefty sip.

"George Criss been around?" Bill asked the barkeep, a man who looked more like a shadow rider than any bartender I'd ever seen. The barkeep only shrugged.

If the town wasn't much to look at, neither was the clientele of this saloon. Now that my eyes had adjusted, all I could see was as scraggly and light-riding a bunch of rattlesnakes as ever held a convention. If it wasn't for the fact that they were all so down on their luck, I do believe they would have slit each other's throats for the price of a drink. There were eight in sight, probably more in the shadows.

One of them, a short, husky fellow, sidled up next to me at the bar.

"What is it you want with George?" he asked.

"Heard he had horses for sale," Bill said, not yet having touched his drink.

And there I was in the middle of a conversation and not doing a lick of talking.

"I heard he was killed six months back."

Cat and mouse is what they were playing, with me caught in the middle of the trap.

"Then he wouldn't be selling horses, would he?" This time Bill pushed that hat of his back on his head and leaned across me, letting the man see the smile on his face.

Bill Barnes let people know who he was when he wanted to, and this was one of those times. It had the desired effect, too, for the man saw Bill's face and turned pale real quick when he recognized whom he was talking to.

"Black Jack, meet George Criss," Bill said with a half smile that had turned deadly, to say the least.

Given my druthers, I'd prefer being shot with an arrow. The damn things thud into you without a sound and it's over with. Firearms will ruin your hearing, particularly when fired in close quarters. I didn't hear the sound of the pistol until the force of the bullet had pushed me facedown on the bar. It caught me high in the back, but even as beefy as my chest is, I knew it was there and painful to boot.

Dying or not, I wasn't about to become the favorite target for whoever it was that had done the shooting. Trouble was I couldn't bring myself upright. Mister Henry was still clenched in my right hand, ready for use if I could ever get up. All I knew about the two shots that followed the one that had gotten me was that they could have been one and the same. The room was being vacated as I looked over my shoulder, and Bill wasn't there anymore. The only two customers left were one fellow sprawled over a tabletop and George What's-His-Name, and both of them were gone beaver.

"You all right?" Bill asked, his eyes darting around the room.

"Silly goddamn question," I muttered, leaning on the bar, but he was gone again by then. The only person left in the saloon was the barkeep and he wasn't looking any too friendly right now, his hand moving toward something under the bar. I brought Mister Henry up level with his chest. "Touch it and you'll be dead before you hit the floor."

He was feeling real confident, this one; he probably already had his hand on the butt of that pistol he kept hidden. Over-confidence can kill a man.

"You look too peaked to pull the trigger, old-timer," the barkeep said with a leer about the same time his hand moved. Daddy always told me to keep my promises, so I did. Flame shot from the barrel of Mister Henry, likely due to all the pure grain alcohol in the air, and that barkeep—or whatever he was—was dead before he hit the floor.

"Smart ass."

I grabbed the bottle of whatever kind of poison I'd been drinking and took a long pull on it. Hell, if I was going to die, it wouldn't make any difference whether I went blind doing it. But if Bill was out there going after what was likely the rest of the male population of this so-called town, he was going to need some help. Like I said, if I was dying, what difference did it make, anyway?

I dug that kerchief out of my back pocket and sloshed it good with the contents of the bottle and stuck it underneath the collar of my buckskins. A good share of that shoulder already felt like it was on fire, but when the alcohol came in contact with my blood and the busted veins it was coming out of . . . well, son, I'll give you my personal guarantee that there wasn't a soul in town that didn't hear me scream like a Crow on the warpath! Not unless they were stone deaf! I meant for the alcohol to keep me from getting infected, but the fact is that all it did was light a bigger fire in me, reminding me that I was indeed alive and in one hell of a lot of pain.

And that made me mad.

I never have cared much for wolves or anything that

hunts in packs, and that was what I was beginning to associate these horse thieves with. Martha used to tell me that love and hate were the two most powerful emotions, and I reckon she was right. There was no woman I would ever love in this world more than I had my Martha. And at the moment there wasn't anyone I hated more than the sons of bitches who'd been the cause of me getting shot. You think I wasn't ready to charge hell with a bucket of water? Bet the farm on it, son, 'cause that's exactly what I did.

One quick gulp of that home brew and then I stepped out through the batwing doors, expecting to die right then and there. And I might have, too, except that there was so much confusion taking place that I don't think I could have caused any more if I'd tried. A half dozen of these yahoos had mounted up and were heading out of town as fast as their nags could carry them. Those that weren't in hiding couldn't tell who was shooting at whom, or so it looked to me. There were a lot of pistols being shot, and one fool took my war bonnet off my head again, which only made me all the madder.

Then I saw him.

Across the street and down the alleyway came Bill, with both pistols out. Whether he did it on purpose or just because he was brave and foolish I'll never know, but he stepped out into the open and, catching sight of both men on either side of him, fired both six-guns at once to each side, dropping each man to the boardwalk.

"Damn fool!" I yelled out and raised Mister Henry at the same time, taking aim in his direction. Can you imagine how he must have felt seeing the only ally he had in this fracas taking a bead on him? It took an instant for all of it to register in his mind before he started shifting those pistols toward me, but that was all I needed. Mister Henry was still in good speaking order and hit the mark. What happened to the head of that fellow running up behind Bill from the alley wasn't pretty at all, but Bill saw it as the man fell backward, his bowie falling to the ground.

"Kelso! Get Kelso!" Bill yelled, pointing to another rider fleeing the scene in haste. He was over a hundred yards away, which must have been why Bill called to me, so I let Mister Henry do my talking for me again. The result was the same, as a part of the bareheaded man's scalp flew off to one side before he tumbled to the ground, dead.

"Damn it, I wanted him alive!" Barnes said, crossing the now deserted street. Except for a handful of dead bodies, it didn't seem like anyone in town wanted to do much associating with us anymore. But I reckon the threat of lead poisoning does that to a man.

I levered a round into Mister Henry just so young William got the idea that the ugliness on my face was exactly what I was feeling inside and nothing less.

"Well, I'm sorry all to hell and gone, mister, but ever since that pilgrim put a slug in my back, I've had a right strong desire to shoot and kill." I said it hard and even, daring him to take up where that smart-ass barkeep had left off. "Comes with being old as the hills, I reckon."

I think the two of us noticed that I was bleeding from both the front and back at about the same time, but it was Bill who got a mite rattled over it.

"Say, shouldn't you be sitting down and getting taken care of?" he asked with genuine concern.

"Likely," I growled, "but as soon as I did, a young pup like you'd no doubt be standing there telling me I'm too old for this sort of thing." Believe me, friend, if age is a state of mind, I could have been the Almighty Himself at the end of the sixth day, as tired as I was feeling all of a sudden.

The mad was pretty much draining out of me as he got me back inside that sorry excuse for a saloon and set me down between a chair and a table. I took a healthy gulp of whatever poison the bottle in front of me contained, while Bill pulled out my bowie and cut away a good share of the upper left corner of my shirt.

"A least it's a clean one," he said after examining the wound. "Stop that bleeding and rest yourself up some, and you'll be good as new before you know it."

"That fella knew you from somewheres, didn't he?" I

asked as he set about stoking a Franklin stove in the far corner of the room. I didn't think I'd ever forget the look of fear on the face of the man whom Bill had called George Criss.

"You could say that." There he was playing games with me again, being elusive as all hell.

"Oh, he knew you, all right," I said, somewhere between gasping and grunting. The pain was intense in my shoulder now. "I've only seen a look like that on one other 'un's face and he knew death was coming to get him, too."

Bill looked at me, nodding slowly. He knew.

"Danny," was all he said, all he had to say. I wondered if I'd ever be rid of that nightmare; wondered then if dying wouldn't be worth it to put an end to it.

"If the pain's too much, grit your teeth and close your eyes, Black Jack. I won't tell anyone you acted like a pained human for once in your life." He was being sarcastic, but I was past caring about sparring with him. It had been a long time since I'd endured such pain and it hadn't been a picnic then, so I took his advice and let my head roll back against the wall, closed my eyes and grit my teeth as he walked away.

It didn't seem like more than a minute when I heard him coming back toward me. I was simply too tired to open my eyes again.

"You're a pretty tough old bastard, ain't you, Black Jack?" he said in that low, soft voice of his.

"Yeah," I said, opening my eyes, and was about to ask him why, when he threw his surprise at me.

The burn of the shot glassful of what passed for drinking whiskey in this establishment couldn't hold a candle to the fire of the red-hot bowie Bill Barnes quickly pressed against the wound opening. He cauterized the wound in doing it, but he also got one hell of an earful of devilish mean cussing as he did.

"That's what I thought," he said as the stink of my own burning flesh made its way into my nostrils and nausea came over me.

"Now you can say you've had a walk through hell, too," was the last thing I heard him say—smiling, too, can you beat it?—before I passed out.

Chapter 10

When I came to, I was facedown on the table the way a man might be after a good drunk, if there is such a thing. The pain in my shoulder, front and back, was unbearable and I had the definite notion that Bill had laid that bowie to my back for cauterization as well. I was weak and feverish and unsure of whether or not I could even stand up straight at the moment, so I lay there for a bit, collecting my thoughts.

Naturally, the first thing I was going to do was kill this Bill Barnes and do it in short order, but I didn't even know where Mister Henry was or whether I had the strength to pick him up if I could locate him.

"William," I called out in a voice that I thought took all my strength but didn't seem to carry too far. Mama did that when we were kids; called us by our full names when she was getting downright serious about something we shouldn't have done in the first place. Young William hadn't pleased me too much in the recent past, either.

There was no reply, for the only ones who heard me were the dead men, and they don't talk back to you—most don't anyway. Tranquility is not a common event in a man's lifetime on the frontier, especially when you've been the places I have, so when you get it you learn to enjoy it. I lay there and tried to make sense of what was going on, but without much success. Maybe I should be settling down with Callie and Robert, I thought; maybe I was getting too old for this kind of life. Maybe . . .

The footsteps on the boardwalk were light and springy, not heavy like mine. Bill, most likely. Yet there wasn't much I could do about visitors in my present state.

"I was hoping you'd be awake," Bill said. "Think you can down some food?" He set a plate of food on the table, and all of a sudden my stomach was telling me it had been some time since it had been fed. He helped me to a chair where I could lean back against the wall some and pushed the table in toward me so I wouldn't have to move that far. The plate had what looked like a handful of bacon slabs and a mess of eggs that had been scrambled, and the cup and pot of coffee he set down were mighty tempting—but there was one thing I had to know first.

"Where's Mister Henry?" The gravel was still there in my voice, but I had a suspicion not all the force was in it.

He nodded toward the bar where I saw the barrel of my rifle sticking out over the end.

"You left me here with no weapon?" True, the man had saved my life and I wasn't acting all too grateful, but you wouldn't be bowing down to kiss the floor, either, if you were in my condition. After all, it was him that got me into this mess.

"Don't hand me that, Hooker. That Tinker is still hanging down your back and you've got your bowie." He was right, for both weapons were in place just as he said, the bowie not having a mark on it. "Besides," he added, glancing at the rifle and back at me, "don't think I didn't know what you'd have in mind once you came to. Now, eat your food."

"Yes, Mama."

He ignored the remark, taking a seat across the table from me. There is something about food that tends to rejuvenate your system. You'd have to find some fancy backseat scientist to explain how it works. All I know is, it does, and it was doing the job now. The fever might be lingering on but the weakness was slowly disappearing, and the confusion and light-headedness were gone by the time I'd finished the meal. Well, the light-headedness, any-way. Young William told another of his tall tales while I ate.

"Got into a fight with a grizzly a few years back," he said. "Had a Colt's with me when I stumbled on him. Emptied all six shots into him and used my bowie to stab him as many times as I could before I died myself." He paused.

"From what they tell me, the bear was laying across me when they found me unconscious, and both of us were bleeding like hell. Nearly tore my arm off, that griz." He paused again, refilling my cup for me. "So I know how you feel, Hooker. I know *exactly* how you feel."

I didn't say much, for it could have happened. Hell, everyone knew about Hugh Glass meeting that griz under about the same circumstances that Bill had described, then crawling half-dead to the nearest help which, by the by, was some ways off. Not an awful lot of men have lived to tell about such stories, and I reckon when they tell them it does stretch the imagination some. But that's how this land is. You can survive the damnedest things, whether by luck or skill, and folks in these civilized communities won't believe you. Now, if you were to tell them a whopper, why, they'd believe every word of it!

"Speaking of storytelling," I said, finishing my coffee, "just who the hell are you, mister?"

"I thought we agreed we wouldn't go into that any-more." Still soft and easy when he spoke, his voice had a firmness to it now.

"No, *you* said we wouldn't talk about it anymore." The force was creeping back into my own tone and I was be-ginning to feel a lot better, despite the pain.

"I told you, old man, don't push it," he said, a real sharp edge to the words this time. "Now, if you think you can walk, there's a livery just down the street with hay that's a helluva lot softer for sleeping on than these floors ever will be."

Outside the saloon I saw that the sun wasn't far from setting. Getting a night's rest would help me more than anything else I could think of right then, so I told him to point in the right direction and I'd be on my way.

"I'll be along directly," he said when he'd done so. "I've got a prisoner to pick up first."

"You mean you actually captured one of the thieves you came after? By the way, whatever happened to the horses?"

"Some of those yahoos made off with the horses when the shooting started, as far as I can tell." He didn't seem either disappointed or happy about it, not that I'd come to expect any different by now, mind you. "And yes, I did manage to take a prisoner. Buffaloed him when the shooting began and tied him up. I think he's one of the horse thieves, although he's not doing any talking."

I made my way to the livery and found that the horses had been taken care of, our saddles and bedrolls set aside. It was tempting to lie down and go to sleep right then, but I had some questions I wanted to ask Bill first and I stood in the doorway waiting for him.

It was approaching dusk when he came down the street, the prisoner walking by his side, hands tied in front of him. The man didn't look any gruffer than any of the other people I'd met in this unfriendly town so far, but then, being tied up never does appeal to a body, I reckon.

They weren't but thirty yards away when the man made a break for it. I don't know why he did it; but as crazy as the world had been getting, it was hard to explain anything anymore. Walking at Bill's right side, he suddenly reached over and yanked the pistol out of the right side of Bill's waistband. As quick as he did it he cocked and fired the gun, but it misfired and he turned to run. He hadn't gone but ten yards when he stopped and turned to take another shot at Bill.

It was one of the damnedest things I ever did see.

By that time, Bill had drawn his second pistol and had a bead on the man, holding the gun in both hands as he took aim. It wasn't seeing Bill's expertness with a pistol that threw me, for he was good, no doubting that. It was the prisoner who, when he turned to fire, had the most

astonished look on his face, much like Criss had—the man
Bill had killed earlier in the day. Like Criss, this one knew
death was coming; knew he had met his match.

Bill shot him through the heart; he had to have for the
man to fall lifelessly to the ground that fast. Then Bill
picked up his gun, not even nudging the body with his toe
to see if he actually had killed him, he was that sure of
himself. Bill left the body there, continuing his now unes-
corted walk to the livery.

"One more took care of," he said nonchalantly as he
walked to his bedroll, a brief smile curling his lips.

I had lost all desire for conversation with the man, and
we spent the next half hour cleaning our weapons in silence. It was sundown by the time we'd finished. Bill adjusted his bedding the way he always did and lay back
against that saddle, the old flop hat covering his face, his
arms crossed over his chest. I studied him in the dim evening light as I set down Mister Henry and prepared my
own bedroll.

Sometimes things will fall into place and seem clear as
day at a moment's notice. I reckon it's your memory working harder than it should that does it. Whatever it is, I had
a whole new realization of the man who called himself Bill
Barnes before I went to sleep that night.

Thinking about him, I remembered the events of the evening, particularly what had taken place here in this barn
and on the street fronting it. Bill was bringing the prisoner
to the livery—although now I couldn't figure out why, since
the man could have been secured anywhere else in this now
deserted town. The horse thief had made a desperate attempt to escape and, in the process, do away with his cap-
tor. Pulling the gun from Bill's near side and the misfire
all seemed in order, events that might and could have happened to anyone. But that look on his face when Bill was
sighting in on him still bothered me.

Then there was the time we spent reloading and caring
for our weapons afterward. I hadn't caught on to it at first
but now it came to mind that after Bill had cleaned and
loaded the gun he had fired and replaced it in his waist-

band, he had done the same with the weapon he'd taken away from the man he'd killed. The cleaning of it was only natural for a frontiersman who wanted a workable weapon on him; it was the loading that now seemed suspicious to me. Bill had loaded all six chambers!

After a while you get familiar with the guns you use, whether long guns or pistols. Fact is, you could be blind and still be able to tell them apart. The Old Sharps and the Hawken I'd used earlier in my life each had a whole different feel than Mister Henry, just as a Colt's Navy is different in heft from the Dragoon or the Army model. More important, you get used to the feeling a gun has when it's loaded and unloaded. Knowing that explained the look on that fellow's face when he brought that gun up the second time. A loaded Navy hefts just about as much as an empty Army model, weightwise. It was only natural to allow for a misfire when he pulled Bill's gun that first time, as fast as things were happening. It was when he turned to fire again that he must have realized that what he was holding was an empty Army Colt and knew he'd been set up to die.

And he did.

I thought I knew him, then, thought I knew this Bill Barnes I'd been riding with. Oh, he was good with a gun and fast and as deadly a pistoleer as I'd ever seen, no question about that. And he could be brave like some I'd only heard of but never seen. He was all of that and I wouldn't deny it. But as I gently laid my body down to rest that night, I thought I'd gained a new insight into Bill Barnes.

He had all the qualities of your storybook hero, Bill did, and in a way I reckon that's fine. But I went to sleep that night knowing for a fact that he was as cold-blooded a killer as I'd ever met in my life.

Chapter 11

We left early the next morning, and I mean *early*. It was more than an hour before daylight and all we had for breakfast was hardtack and jerked beef. But foremost in our minds was the knowledge that those yahoos weren't going to stay away from their hangout long, especially if they could find some hard liquor, a feat which is never hard for a crowd like that.

So we left before dawn.

"Where do you think you're going?" I growled when we reached the edge of town, recognizing it as the east side. As for growling, well, son, you would, too, if you hadn't had the chance to get some coffee inside you and felt as full of pain as I did.

"We're going to find you a doctor, Hooker." Bill Barnes was in the same temperament by the sound of him. We'd gotten up and saddled in silence, neither one of us saying spit to the other. That meant that either Barnes was getting as tired of me as I was of him or that hot black coffee is as important out here to a man as the weapons and ammunition he uses. I suspicion it was a mixture of both.

"Doctor!"

"Yes," he said, and I could tell he wasn't any more pleased with the decision than I was. "You ain't any more of a doctor than I am, old man, and that wound of yours needs treating." There was more than disappointment in his voice when he said, "I oughtta leave you here

to die, but you stood by me so I'm taking you to a farm-
house fifteen miles down the road. I know the folks there
and they'll take care of you.''

You'd get no argument from me that my wound needed
some looking at, but I was damned if I was going to admit
it to this youngster.

''Never would've happened if we'd been in the Shinin'
Mountains. Never!''

''What are you talking about?''

''Been shot many a time in them mountains. No, sir,
never would have happened.''

''What the hell are you talking about, old man?'' he
asked again.

''Meat don't spoil in the Rockies, son. No, sir.''

I started the horse to moving, then reined in after a couple of steps, Bill doing the same. I reckon he knew I'd go
to that farm eventually. There was just one matter I had to
straighten out with him first.

''One more thing, *sonny*,'' I said, emphasizing the last
word. He'd learned about riding on my left, Bill had, so
he was on my right side now as I spoke. But that didn't
make any difference.

''What is it, *old man*?'' He was throwing the same insult
right back at me. Like I said, it didn't make any difference.

I brought Mister Henry across the front of me until the
side of the barrel whacked into the upper part of Bill Barnes'
chest, then moved it just a mite up to his Adam's apple.

''Next son of a bitch calls me an old man is gonna die,
and you ain't no exception to the rule. Comprende,
amigo?''

He just barely said yes in that soft voice he had—or
maybe it was Mister Henry up against his throat that made
him speak that way. Either way I think he got the message.
Of course, my stomach got a bit queasy, too, toward the
end there, for although I didn't know for sure, it being as
dark as it was, I could have sworn I heard the cocking of
one of his Colts as I spoke.

Two hours later the sun was up and it had the look of
being a scorcher. We'd walked the horses more than we

had ridden them, the pain in my side getting more unbearable as the day went on. I knew it wouldn't be long before I felt about as weak as a pup, but that wasn't what bothered me most. Thirsty? Hoss, I could have stood at the mouth of the Colorado River and drunk it dry at spring thaw and it wouldn't have filled me up at all. Not a'tall!

"How much further is this place?"

"Five, six miles." He grinned as if he enjoyed seeing me in this condition. "What's the matter, Hooker, you want to show 'em how?"

"These mounts ain't gonna die at a good five-mile run, son, but the way I'm feeling now I got a notion I might." It couldn't have been more than a whisper in which I spoke, my mouth was that dry.

He leaned across his saddle to me, pressing a hand against my forehead, then dismounted.

"Fever's catching up with you again," he said. "Think you got enough strength to hang onto that rifle of yours and the reins at the same time?"

"Ain't but one way to find out."

He wrapped the reins around my big fist, closing it tight around them, and mounted up again.

"Give him your heels, Hooker," was all he said before I heard the thunder of his own horse's hooves gallop away. I did what he suggested, not sure whether I'd make it or not.

I almost passed out a couple of times during that ride, although you'd think that riding at a fast pace five miles wouldn't take that long. For me it was forever.

"Johnny, fix me up my spare room out to the barn," was the next thing I heard Bill saying as we came to a stop. "Otis, I've got a man that's hurt bad and needs fixing. Miss Darlene still around?" There was a sense of urgency in his voice, and whoever these folks were they did just like Bill Barnes said.

I focused my eyes on a balding, potbellied man in work clothes standing in front of a cabin, a pleasant smile on his face. "How are you doing there, old man?" he said, looking at me with that same smile.

The fire must have shot into my eyes and scared the living hell out of him, for his own eyes got big and round, like his face. Whether he knew it or not, I was about to slide off that horse and show him a thing or two about us old bastards. I was going to kill him!

I slid off the horse, all right, but it wasn't my feet that hit the ground first.

It was my face.

"Are you really as mean as Mister Barnes says?"

I heard the voice before I saw who it was coming from, but by that time my right hand had balled up into a fist. The left side of me . . . well, I wasn't sure I could move it at all. But when my eyes focused on Johnny, the boy Bill had given orders to, it didn't seem to matter so much. Hell, who'd want to hurt a ten-year-old boy as tousle-haired and innocent as this one looked? I did my best to smile, although I wasn't all that sure I could speak. The boy must have noticed and was gone and back in an instant with a tin cup of cool water to pour down me once he'd propped my head up to just the right angle.

" 'Bliged, son." I was enjoying the clean taste, but the lad was still waiting for an answer to his question, standing there silent and still. "Yes, I can get tarnational mean," I said. His smile was instantly replaced by the beginnings of a frown. "But, shoot, boy, you would, too, ary you'd ar-keetecked the Shinin' Mountains the way I done!"

"Really?" His eyes were wide in awestruck wonder.

Not that I ever mind stretching the blanket, mind you, but I had other needs right then.

"You got any more of that Adam's Ale handy?" He squinted, unsure of just what I was referring to, then glanced at the empty tin cup and knew I meant the water.

"Oh. Yes, sir." Again he was gone and back in a wink, as eager to please as any youngster that age. "I'll get Ma," he said, handing me the cup.

"How 'bout handing me Mister Henry afore you go."

"Sir?" He was puzzled, but most of them usually are.

"That long gun across the room there." I nodded my

head. "The repeater rifle." Once I had the rifle in hand, he disappeared from sight.

The water was good, but it felt more reassuring to have Mister Henry by my side. I had been laid down in some sort of bed—it was too soft to be made of earth—that was stuck back in the corner of the barn. I still had my bottoms on but my shirt had been removed, and part of the reason I couldn't move my left shoulder and side was the tightness of the bandaging that had been done to me.

"Well, Mr. Hooker, I'm glad to see you're back among the living," a short, middle-aged woman said, rounding the entrance to the barn and heading straight for me. She had the same pleasant smile about her that her husband had. She was a plain-looking woman, who had the time she'd been on the frontier written on her face. "And how do you feel, sir?"

"Empty, ma'am," I said, "and sore as hell. Oh, pardon me, ma'am," I said as an afterthought. But that didn't seem to bother her much.

"It would seem you've chosen the right time to wake up, Mr. Hooker. My husband will be in from the fields shortly, and I expect that Bill and my daughter will return from their ride directly for supper."

"Right hospitable, ma'am," I said, a smile forming on my own face as I swung my feet to the floor, not feeling as hard put to move as I had before.

"You're smiling, Mr. Hooker," she said, the mischief in her own eyes coming out. "Why?"

"Well, ma'am," I said, bringing myself to my full height and hefting my rifle as I looked down at her, "truth to tell, if you hadn't offered a meal, I was planning on going out and shooting one my own self." My stomach growled.

"I see." The woman smiled, shook her head, and walked back to the cabin.

I found my jacket and spent a clumsy minute putting it on before heading for the smell of her cooking. I never could understand why those Indians went around bare-chested all the time. Hell of a way to catch cold if you ask me. Or maybe I wasn't used to being without my buck-skins, top and bottom. When I walked inside the cabin, the woman caught a whiff of my jacket and made a face.

"Been in the barn too long, have I, ma'am?" That was about as polite and civilized as you'd see me get.

"Mr. Hooker, you've been *outside* too long," was her reply. She disappeared from the oven for a moment, entered a separate room, and returned shortly with a man's cotton shirt. "Why don't you save your jacket for the trail and put this on instead?"

"Yes, ma'am. I surely will." And did exactly as she suggested. I was none too keen on wearing anything other than my buckskins, but I learned a long time ago that you never get on the wrong side of the cook, as it tends to result in smaller portions being served. If you know what I mean.

As it turned out, Emma was her name and she was just full of news about the territory and questions about where I'd been and the rest of the world in general. Not that you could blame a person out here on the plains. Why, I was two years in the mountains once before I stopped a family heading down the Santa Fe Trail when I came out of the Rockies. Had them talking for a day and a half about what was going on in the civilized world—even found out who the new president was! So as long as she had the coffee to spare, I didn't mind palavering at all while the rest of the family drifted in.

But it was the woman's daughter, Darlene, who caught my eye as I stood in the doorway when she and Bill rode in. Couldn't have been more than fifteen or so, but you could tell she was full-grown all right, and I'm not talking about *height*, son. She had auburn hair and the prettiest smile I'd seen since . . . since Martha. Or Callie. I could tell that this was how Emma had looked years ago when she was her daughter's age. Did you ever notice how a woman who has brown eyes and is taken with a man tends to look softer and more helpless than most? Mama was like that and passed it on to Callie I reckon, for she's the only one of us Hookers who has brown eyes. The boys all have blue eyes.

"It's nice to see you up and about, Mr. Hooker," she said as Bill helped her dismount and took the horses away.

"Ma'am, the sight of you would give any man tanglefoot of the tongue sure as could be, so I ain't even going to comment except for saying one thing." She was beginning to blush, likely in expectation, as I stood there for a moment admiring her.

"Well, Mr. Hooker, what is it?" She smiled.

But it wasn't to the young lady I spoke. Leaning against the doorway, I looked over my shoulder. "Emma, you got one beauteous daughter."

"I'll say," I heard Bill agree as he came from the barn, but it was Emma standing next to that hot stove I was looking at. Her cheeks were as flushed as her daughter's, and I thought I saw a tear roll down the side of her cheek— it had been some time since she'd been reminded of what she'd once looked like.

"Ma?" little Johnny asked, not sure what was taking place.

"It's just the heat, son," she said, tossing me a glance, "just the stove and all."

"Yup," I said to Bill as he walked inside, "I'm meaner than hell."

Supper was pretty tame as far as the conversation went, although it didn't take much to see Bill Barnes was making Darlene the center of his attention. He was as kind and smiling as could be, a far cry from what I'd experienced of him earlier.

I found out that I had been unconscious for nearly a day after Darlene had bandaged me up. Like I said, I've been shot before, and after a while your body adjusts to it, I reckon, for what with the afternoon coffee and the meal I was now eating, I could begin to feel my strength coming back. I knew I wouldn't be fighting any mountain lion real soon, but I wasn't light-headed anymore, nor was the fever there, and except for the damned pain, I could get around fine. Maybe another day or so of rest and I'd be all right.

There were a couple of hours of daylight left when we left the table, and for Johnny I reckon they were as important as the rest of the day had been, for his mother let him sit out front with the rest of the men rather than making him help with the women's chores inside. His pa did some storytelling, then excused himself to check on some of his farm tools before turning in. That was when Johnny finagled his ma into letting him sit up with Bill and me in the barn for a while before we turned in our own selves.

"What's it like out west?" Johnny asked on the way to the barn. "What's it like out near those mountains you built, Mr. Hooker?" That drew a raised eyebrow from Bill but it didn't stop me.

"Let me tell you, son, it was a job!" I said, wiping my hand across my brow as though I'd just completed it. "Why, I had to go all the way from Canada to Old Mexico to do it. Found every rock there was on these plains, you see, and carried 'em all out west and let 'em drop when I got tired. By then, why, it was close to the middle of summer, so I waited for it to get good and hot and wouldn't you know it, those rocks melted and became one big, gigantic range of mountains. Then the winter come and froze 'em solid and they ain't moved since!"

"Really?" The boy was awestruck again. "What did you call 'em, Mr. Hooker?"

"Why, the Rockies, of course!" Even Bill laughed at that one.

"Tell me more, Mr. Hooker."

"Well, uh . . . in a bit, son. Gotta clean Mister Henry now. Maybe young William here can tell you a tale or two; he appears to have been around some."

"Why do you call your rifle Mister Henry?" Johnny asked.

"Yeah, Black Jack," Bill added, "I been meaning to ask you about that. How come?"

"I'll tell you something, boys; I've been around for some time now. Ain't much of my life I'd trade for anyone else's, I like it that much. But there's places I've been that no man will ever likely go, and being there, well, at times it makes you lonely for all you left behind. Your horse and your gun are the best friends you'll ever have in a land like that, so you start treating 'em like they were pards to you.'' I looked at the Henry repeater in my hand. ''Sometimes you even give 'em names like they were humans. I know it's crazy, boys, but it's the way of things, like it or not.''

I fell silent then, remembering times that should have been forgotten long ago, cleaning my rifle as I did so. Maybe I *was* a crazy old man, hell, I didn't know. It was having all that time to think that made a man stir-crazy, for he started asking questions that he didn't have the answers for, and when you're by yourself that can be dangerous. In more ways than one.

''You're living in part of those plains Hooker claims he rid of all the rocks, Johnny,'' Bill said with a smile. ''But you ask your pa and I'll guarantee he's found every one of those that Black Jack missed right under the surface of the back forty.''

''But, what's it like out there?'' the boy asked, an urgency in his voice.

''It's big, Johnny.'' Bill looked off into the distance as he spoke, and I knew he was seeing things that had already passed in his life, too. ''There's trails that only an animal can follow and ones only a man would dare blaze. Land that stretches as far as the eye can see, valleys and mountains that look like they'll never end, depending on whether you're standing on top looking down or on the bottom looking up. There's rivers as wide as you could imagine, and you know what?''

''What?''

''They trickle right down into streams not bigger than your arm.''

''Is that true?'' Johnny asked me.

''Sure is.''

''There's animals out there that are twice as big as Hooker and a whole lot friendlier,'' Bill went on. I gave both of them a stoic stare that turned into a gentle grin.

''And Injuns?''

Bill nodded seriously. ''Yup. And bad men, too. Outlaws, thieves, killers, why—'' Then he stopped abruptly, giving Johnny a knowing glance and me a curious one. Johnny knew something about him that I didn't, and Bill wasn't telling, that much I did catch, whether they knew it or not. Bill, he was a sharp one, I'll give him that.

"Say, did I ever tell you about Old John Colter and how he used to hunt beaver before the likes of Hooker, here, took to trapping?" Bill asked.

"No, sir."

"Old Colter, he used to sneak up near a pack of beaver that were trying to cut down one of them trees in the Petrified Forest, and of course they never could, so all he did was stand off to the side while they made their attempt. Then he'd take aim with that rifle of his and shoot behind the beaver, ricochet the bullet off the inside of his teeth, and kill him without destroying the fur at all!"

"Really?" Johnny was looking at me again for confirmation.

"He's telling the story, son. Strangest story about Colter is the way he died. Camping out in the dead of winter in the Sawatch, he was. Freezing cold it was, too. Well, Johnny, he gets up one morning and his fire's 'bout out, and he walks outside and falls directly down in the stream he's camped in front of. Gets hisself tarnational wet from the waist down.''

"Then what happened?"

"Why, his buckskins froze stiff quicker'n you could blink an eye. Falls down, he does, and breaks them pants into a thousand pieces of ice and scratches his legs all up. Only thing saved him was the frost. Yes, sir. Froze them wounds shut something fierce.'' I was silent for a moment, making the boy think. Then he caught on.

"But you said he died!"

"Oh, he did, Johnny, he did.'' More silence.

"But how?"

"Why, the spring thaw come and he bled to death.'' That got a laugh out of both of them, but that's the purpose of a good story. Still, I doubted if I would give Joe Meek or Jim Bridger any competition.

"I wish I was a couple of years older," the boy said, a bit of sadness filling his voice. "I'd like to go out there and do all the things you two have. I wish it wasn't today."

He yawned now, getting tired, leaning against Bill as he sat next to him on the hay.

"I'll tell you what, Johnny," I said, looking out the entrance into what was now the night, "I done some thinking on that a long time back. Actually, if you think about it, there ain't an awful lot wrong with today. Fact is, somewhere down the trail you're going to look back on today as being one helluva long time ago!"

When no response came I looked at the boy, only to see him fast asleep, his head sort of balanced against Bill's big strong shoulder.

"Better get him inside, I reckon," Bill said, taking Johnny in his arms as effortlessly as if he were a newborn. Heading toward the house he said, "You sure can tell some tall ones, Black Jack."

"Tall ones?" I gave him a look in the darkness that said I wasn't sure if he was complimenting me or implying that what I said had been as tall as a Texas lie.

"Yes. You know, Colter and all that."

Johnny's mother opened the door as Bill and I approached.

"Son, what I know about John Colter ain't exactly tall tales. You see, he married a young lady named *Nancy Hooker*."

Bill gave me a doubtful glance as he carried Johnny inside. It didn't take but a few seconds, but that gave Emma enough time to say her piece.

"You're a strange man, Mr. Hooker, a strange man."

"No ma'am, Miss Emma," I replied as Bill passed back out through the doorway. "I may be a mite old, but this 'un"—I yanked a thumb over my shoulder at him—"he's the strange one. Yes'm."

With that we bedded down for the night, doing so in silence now that Johnny was gone. I had a few stray thoughts just before I drifted off into sleep and they were about Bill. How could a man as cold-blooded as this one had been a couple of days back be as playful and kind with a young girl like Darlene or as much a storyteller to a boy like Johnny as he had tonight? There was something complex about him, something that only a few knew about and weren't saying.

No, sir, it wasn't me that was *strange* by any means. It was Bill Barnes.

Chapter 12

We stayed one more day before leaving, me so I could get more of my strength back, and Bill—well, young William did what seemed like a whole day's riding with Darlene. I had a notion that boy was quite the lady's man when he wasn't out shooting up people and places. It was past daybreak when Bill Barnes and I mounted up with full stomachs in front of the cabin.

Sometimes it's hard to leave. You get attached to some people, even over a period of two or three days, and you wish you didn't have to move on but you know you have to. Things work out that way at times.

"Well," I said after a long silence, "I reckon we'd better git. Got some ground to cover."

"Miss Emma, you are about the best cook I've come across since my Martha; if I had the time, I'd stay for no other reason than that." The woman blushed.

"Can I go, too?" Johnny suddenly blurted out, surprising all of us.

"Johnny!" his father said in embarrassment.

"Oh, you don't want to go with us, son," Bill said. "Why, old Hooker and me just get in one scrape after another and pull each other's bacon outta the fire." Then, with clear understanding on his face, he added, "Believe me, I know how it is to be between hay and grass. Just don't seem like it'll ever end. But don't you worry, Johnny, I'll be back again, maybe sooner than you think."

"But what about the West?" The boy had a downtrodden look about him now, and he was kicking the dirt. "I ain't *never* gonna get out west."

"Johnny," I said, throwing a curious glance at him, "you remember what Bill and me was a-telling you the other night?"

"Why, sure! How could I forget?"

"You really oughtta think on it some, son."

"Huh?" he frowned.

I pointed east, then west toward the expanse of land that put this cabin in a barren spot of wilderness.

"Land that stretched as far as the eye could see, ain't that what Bill was telling you?"

"Yes, sir, but—"

"Well, what do you think this is, son!" I roared in true mountain-man fashion. It startled him, and he quickly gazed in both directions, likely wondering what in the world he'd missed.

"Don't you see, Johnny, boy? You're on the far side of the Mississippi, lad! *This is the West!*"

Again he looked in both directions, then looked at his pa in pure speechlessness.

"Well, now, son, I never had thought of it that way," Otis said, "but I do believe the man's right."

"Better git your wits about you if you're going to survive in this land, son." I said it as if I was Jim Bridger himself talking to a new pilgrim that had joined the trapping party and I think Johnny believed it. Better yet, he liked it.

"You bet, Black Jack," the boy said, smiling. "Next time you come by I'll know everything there is to know about this land."

"We'll see, son," I said in a half-doubting manner, "we'll see. You just make sure that along with all that scouting you get you some work done around this camp. And always remember, son."

"Yes, sir?" he said, eagerly.

I winked at Emma. "Always get in good with the cook."

* * *

That must have been the first time that Bill Barnes and
I had left a place without threatening to kill someone else
if not each other, for we were both smiling when we rode
off.

My shoulder and side would be stiff for some time to
come, but I'd been through worse, so we headed for the
nearest military post that Bill knew of, one of I don't know
how many that had sprung up on the Kansas and Missouri
frontiers since this damn-fool war had started. About the
only real reason I was going along with him to the post
was to see if the sutler might have any extra .44s for Mister
Henry. Lord only knew what would crop up next in this
land.

One of the things I hadn't liked about this war from the
start was that you couldn't tell who was fighting for what.
Oh, there were bunches of soldiers stationed all over the
place, but I'll be damned if I could ever get a straight
answer out of any one of them as to just whose side he was
on. Of late there had been an outfit going around by the
name of Jennison's Jayhawkers, that was supposedly fighting for the Union cause. I didn't care for them any more
or less than I did for the others, but one thing was sure the
afternoon Bill Barnes and I rode into that Union camp. For
once I got a straight answer from a couple of those yahoos;
it wasn't what I wanted to hear, but it was the truth. I made
certain of that.

Army camps never have served the kind of liquor a body
needs to cut the dust after a long ride, but this was no time
to be choosy, so Bill said he'd buy the first round; something about knowing the bartender. The bar wasn't any
more permanent than the living quarters in this camp, so I
wasn't too surprised when the fellow tending it pulled out
a bottle of clear liquid that looked like it contained diamondback venom that had been diluted with two-hundred-
proof grain alcohol. You want a fast, cheap drunk, son,
you just drink a cup full of that poison and they'll carry
you out over the last survivor's shoulder. That I guarantee.
Bill was sniffing the brew, likely getting his nostrils used

to it, while I went ahead and took a gulp, then held fast to what passed for a bar top while the fire started below.

Like I said, women are always getting me in trouble, and it was then I heard one of these Jennison lads who shared the bar with us start up a right interesting conversation.

"I tell you, Buck," he was saying to his friend, "a man can get just about anything he wants to out of this war, ain't it true?"

His friend, a man just as near drunk and looking just as ugly, leered back at him knowingly. "I'll say. Fly the right colors and you can even find a woman or two, whether she likes it or not." As mannerless as these two seemed, I'd have bet the whole Rocky Mountain range that if they ever had a woman it would be by taking her rather than by her choice.

"Not in Lawrence, you won't," the first one said. "They ain't none left there." He chuckled in a menacing way but you can bet it wasn't his laugh I had any interest in. No, sir.

"Lawrence, you say," I said, swinging Mister Henry around to the man's throat. Let's just say I wasn't feeling any too friendly.

"Hey, back off, mister," the man said, gulping hard, "I didn't do nothing to you."

"True 'nough, sonny, but if I don't get the right answers, I may be doing something to you. Now what's this about women and Lawrence?"

Either this fellow had had too much panther juice or he was feeling right gamey that day, for even with Mister Henry stuck in his throat he looked back at me meaner than hell.

"Our conversation ain't none of your business, you old—"

"I wouldn't call him nothing *old*, mister," Bill said suddenly, cutting the man off, "unless it was old hoss. As it is, he may kill you for the hell of it, but you remind him of his age and he's gonna kill you for sure."

"I'd listen right hard, if I was you, pilgrim," I said. He

had the look of having been on the frontier long enough to know his way around, so I knew good and well he didn't like what I'd called him. Not one bit. But I wasn't taking a notion to striking up a friendship with this tough anyway, so I pushed the barrel of Mister Henry a tad harder into his throat, and his face got a mite tamer until he took notice of what I was saying. "I got a sister in Lawrence, sonny, so I hope you're stretching the blanket some, 'cause if I found she come to harm, I ain't even gonna ask who done it. I'm a coming for you!"

It would take some time for that alcohol to get out of his system but his mind sobered up real quick.

"I ain't touched your sister, mister," he said in a lower voice. "It was just . . . talk, just talk." He grinned sheepishly. "You know."

"What's this 'bout Lawrence, then?" Mister Henry didn't move one bit.

"It was a guerrilla band, that Quantrill fella, they say. Him and his men burned Lawrence to the ground. Wasn't more'n a day ago, I swear. I ain't lying, mister, honest."

I lowered the rifle barrel to his chest, letting him breathe enough to get some color back in his face.

"You'd better not be, pilgrim, or I won't be this hospitable next time." I spit it out, letting him know I didn't care for him or his kind, honest or not.

Drinking the rest of that Taos Lightning didn't even touch bottom on me, for all I could think of was what had happened to Callie, if what this yahoo had said was right. She was in trouble or, God forbid, dead, and that meant I had to go. The only pain I was feeling then was for my sister. Without a word I turned to leave; I wasn't going to ask Bill Barnes for any help at all. This was family, something I had to do by myself. I hadn't taken but two steps when I heard Bill.

"Hooker!"

My back was to them as the shot went off but nothing hit me as I swung Mister Henry around in a half circle to my right and laid the barrel up alongside the tough who'd all of a sudden gotten his courage back. He had a knife in

his hand at waist level and would have run me through if
Bill hadn't warned me. The bullet, I now saw, had been
from Bill's gun and had disarmed my attacker's friend as
he'd pulled his pistol. Soon the knife lay on the floor, and
the drunk who'd held it had a knot aside his head and a
trickle of blood running down his ear.

"Smart ass," was all I said, looking down at him.

Again I turned to leave but was stopped this time by a
gentle hand on the arm as Bill gave me a concerned look.

"Where you going, Black Jack?"

"Jesus, Mary, and Joseph!"

"Well?" He was determined.

"You know, Barnes, for a smart man you sure do ask
some dumb questions."

Then I pulled loose from him and left. . . .

Chapter 13

You can smell a big fire from a long way off if you're downwind of it. But Lawrence, Kansas, had a smell all its own that I would never forget, never in my lifetime. It wasn't only the odor of burned wood and goods and such. Mixed in with it was the putrid stink that is the result of the human body being burned right along with those goods. My horse reared at the stench, as taken aback at it as I was, but I urged him on, my only thought being to find Callie, Robert, and Sarah.

The place looked like hell warmed over, the liveliest things being the few wary survivors picking through the charred remains of what had once been their homes and their businesses. Suddenly my feeling of urgency was gone for I knew there was no way on earth that I could undo what these people had experienced. I gave my mount the rest he deserved, walking him through town to the far side where I hoped I'd find something left of my own kin.

The house that the town had helped raise for Callie and Robert was burned except for the front porch. Sarah's home hadn't fared any better, and the barn . . . well, the horses were lucky if they'd gotten out before it went up in flames. Like I said, I'd seen people milling about as I rode through the town, likely looking for the remains of someone or something. The dead I'd seen were mostly men, a lot of men. Those who were left had their sleeves rolled up and were helping out as best they could to assist those in need.

Now I could see movement to my rear, between the ruins of the main house and the barn. When I dismounted, Sarah came flying around the corner at me.

"Ezra! Oh, it was terrible, terrible, terrible!" she yelled out, finally drowning her own voice in my chest and holding on for dear life. It didn't add any comfort to the pain I was feeling and I never had cared for the woman all that much, but like I said, son, us Hookers are strong on family, and I do believe that I'd have held her until hell froze over if that was how long she took to cry herself out.

"Where's Callie?" I asked in as soft a voice as I ever spoke in, when she was through crying.

Sarah looked back toward the corner of the house she had rounded and that was all I needed to know. I had never been so scared in all my life, except for that once, and right now taking on the whole Blackfoot nation would have been easy compared to what I had to face around the back side of Sarah's house. I slowly released her and began the longest walk in my life, as much sweat forming on my forehead as I went as when I'd been feverish. But I had to know.

A small aid station had been set up to the rear of Sarah's house; a dozen or more cots were set up there for men and women alike, and others were lying on the ground.

"Just a minute, friend," a man in a white shirt, his sleeves rolled back, said, "you can't go in there. Those are my—"

"Outta my way." Growl? Son, I could've fought a grizzly right then, cut his liver out and fed it to him while he died! I pushed the man away with my left hand. It was the first time I'd used it since being shot and it didn't hurt all that bad anymore. Or maybe it was the hurt I was feeling inside that took my mind off physical pain. I walked slowly down the center of the two rows of cots, looking for my sister but not seeing her. Halfway through, I lost my patience.

"Callie!" I yelled, but there was no answer. "Callie!"

I heard footsteps behind me and swung around. Mr. White Shirt was running down the aisle after me.

"Please! Don't go any further! I beg you! These are my patients. I'm a doctor. Please!"

"How'd you like to join 'em, son?" I said, bringing Mister Henry up into his stomach area. This was the wrong time to even *think* about making a suggestion to me, much less to *tell* me what he thought! He turned pale in the face and fell silent, and I went back to my business.

She was all the way in the back, the last one in the row, lying on the ground on a blanket or two, another covering her. Her face was bruised and several teeth were missing. Her eyes were black and blue, and there was a fear that I'd never seen before in them. She spotted me and grabbed the blanket, pulling it as close to her throat as possible.

"Callie, it's me, Ezra," I said in a low voice, kneeling down beside her. "Everything's gonna be all right."

But she knew better. Things would never be the same again for my sister, and suddenly her eyes went wild and she screamed and clawed at me the way a she-panther does. She screamed and screamed and screamed in pure madness. I dropped my rifle then and I held her, knowing it wouldn't do any good; maybe I was doing it more for me than for her. When her crying subsided, I gently lay her back down and covered her up as a shadow loomed behind me and I looked up to see Robert. There was a bandage on his right arm, which was in a makeshift sling, and another around his head.

"She was raped."

I wanted answers then, answers to questions that were coming to me faster than I could find words for them, answers I wasn't sure I wanted to hear. I stood up, facing him, wanting to know why he hadn't died protecting his woman like he should.

"How could you people let it happen, Robert? Are you civilized folk that easy to do in?" I shook my head in despair. "You're sorry, Robert, the whole lot of you. You'd never make it in the Rockies."

I turned to go when he called my name. When I faced him he hit me with his good hand, knocking me to the ground flat on my back. Not many men can do that, but that shows you what rage will do to a body.

"I'm tired of your ways, you pompous *old man*." There it was, hoss, those words again. I was halfway to rising when he said them and had Mister Henry pointed at him by the time they were out of his mouth. "That's your answer to everything, isn't it, Hooker? If they don't conform to your ways, just shoot them." He took a step closer to the rifle barrel and his chest made contact. "Well, go ahead, Hooker, shoot if you like. I'm not worth much to the world without Callie now anyway, so go on." The man absolutely did not care.

"If you wasn't my sister's husband I would shoot you, Robert." It was hard to say it in a calm voice but I did my best. I lowered Mister Henry and there was a bit of silence for a moment as the two of us just stared at one another in anger.

"Don't you see, man, there were four hundred of them!" he finally said. "*Four hundred!* I was in the store and Callie was home, that's why I couldn't get to her." He paused, the anger in him growing. "You have to realize, Hooker, that we don't all go around carrying rifles and knives like you do."

"Well, maybe you should."

He ignored the comment.

"They set torches to every building they could get near. I passed out rifles and pistols to everyone who could get into my store before it was set afire, Hooker, so don't say that we didn't put up a fight!" The anger in him overflowed and he took a step forward, grabbing a fistful of my shirt. "A hundred and fifty men died out in those streets, Hooker. Nobody sat back and let it happen."

"Take your hand off'n my shirt, son, or I'm going to forget you're kin and make the rest of you feel the way your arm does." I said it slow and deliberate, letting him know that he wasn't the only one madder than hell. His hand dropped to his side.

It struck me then right out of the blue, and I frowned as

I glanced at the rubble that had once been the barn, then back at Robert.

"The boy, Jaime. What happened to him?" I'd been so concerned about my own kin that I'd clean forgotten about the boy I'd left behind with them.

"I don't know," he said. "Someone said they thought they saw a youngster being carried off by the raiders that hit our town."

"That so." It couldn't have been Jaime they saw. That much I knew for sure, for the boy was too feisty, too independent to be taken that easily.

I walked toward the smoldering barn. The stench of death was coming from it too, and outside its entrance was the body of a man whose lower half had been burned, leaving only the bullet in his heart and the anguish on his face as evidence of his one-time existence. The odor was stronger here than in most of this area, and it crossed my mind that there might be more than just this one hombre who had died raiding Lawrence. What stuck in my mind was that I *knew* this fellow, knew him from somewhere. Independence? One of those Rebs that Barnes and I had run up against? Where? Maybe there were more clues inside; another one I'd recognize, making it easier to track these sons of bitches down, for that I would. They'd never be able to find a rattlesnake nest or a hole in the wall small enough or far enough away to escape the likes of Ezra Jackson Hooker. No, sir!

Then I saw him, and everything started coming back from way back when. That nightmare I couldn't get away from was coming to life in full daylight now!

"*God damn it!*" I yelled, and if it didn't echo off those Rocky Mountains even from Lawrence, Kansas, well, friend, then I'm losing my lung power! I looked to the heavens where my Maker was and, in just as strong a voice, yelled again. "*Ain't you ever gonna leave me alone?*"

"What is it?" Robert asked, suddenly at my side. Then he saw him too. "Oh, my God!"

It was Jaime, or the remains of him after the fire. The boy had listened good to those stories I'd told him, that he had. Take the high ground, I'd told him, always take the high ground in a fight. Jaime had done just that. When Quantrill and his men had swept into Lawrence, the boy had grabbed up a pistol, the same one still clenched in his fist, and headed for the hayloft. It seemed reasonable to assume that he had killed the man I'd first seen. Whether he had gotten off any other shots, I didn't know. Likely he had been killed outright by the bullet that had torn away half of the back of his skull. A sack of grain had fallen atop him, the only thing to save part of his identity.

There was a moment of silence as we both stared down in shock at the boy.

"I wasn't ever going tell this story, Robert," I said, still staring down at Jaime, "and if you ever tell anyone about this, I'll kill you, I swear I will."

"I understand." Maybe he did. Or maybe it was the tear that rolled down into my beard and disappeared that convinced him. It was all I would allow.

"You remember that story I told you 'bout them Blackfoot and how they test a body's bravery?" All the while I spoke I was looking down into the hollowed-out eyes of Jaime.

"Yes, I remember."

"Got that firsthand, I did."

"I don't understand."

"Had a young boy with us when we went off one year to the Shinin' Mountains. Musta been thirty years ago. No more than a kid, would you believe it? A year, maybe two older than Jaime was, and he had the worst itch of wanting to be a man that you ever saw. Daniel was his name. Danny we called him. Had gumption too; would've made a fine mountain man."

"Would have?"

"Would have. Wasn't but five of us in the group that fall and wouldn't you know we got into a scrape in Blackfoot country. One of 'em got close 'nough to take Danny. Just like I told you, Robert, them Blackfoot got devilish ways. The four of us, we snuck up on 'em not a day later. Couldn't help but find 'em, the way that boy was screaming. Just like Callie. Fierce, it was. They had him staked out when we got to the camp, like I told you, Robert, and they'd pulled 'bout four or five one-inch strips of his skin clean off his chest. He was covered in his own blood. Young Daniel, he wasn't all that tough after all, for he was begging 'em to take his life.

"There was seven Blackfoot there, Robert. I killed three of 'em by my own hand, and you can believe every one of 'em died. Anyway, that's why Sarah hates me so, claims I led Danny to his death." I had relived every moment of that day while I told it, all the while looking at another boy I'd led to death.

"I'm sorry for you, Ezra," Robert said, the contempt now gone from his voice. "But surely Sarah couldn't hold that against you all these years. After all, he was only a boy who—"

"He wasn't just any boy, Robert. *He was my brother.*" With this last, I faced him, and out of the corner of my eye spotted Sarah standing not six feet away, her eyes shockingly huge, a hand across her mouth to stifle her cries.

"Oh, my God," were the only words to come from her as tears streamed down her cheeks and she rushed to me, burying her face in that weatherbeaten buckskin jacket of mine that she hated so much. "Please forgive me, Ezra," she mumbled. After a moment I held her at arm's length, feeling somehow freed of a burden I had been carrying too long.

"Dry as it gets out here, you oughtta save the water for your flower bed."

"But Ezra, you just said he was dead when you returned," she said. "You never explained how it happened, not like you did just now."

"I'll sit down and tell you all about it one day, Sarah," I said, glancing at the sky and looking for the sun. "Right now I've got to do some scouting."

"Whatever for?" she asked, purely bewildered.

"Wolves run in packs, Sarah, and what I'm 'bout to scout up is a pack of wolves."

"Where are you going?" Robert asked.

I shook my head in disbelief.

"There sure do seem to be a lot of people asking awful stupid questions around here of late, Robert," I said. "Yes, sir."

I left them at that and mounted my horse.

"I'll pray for you, Ezra," Sarah said, actually smiling for the first time since I'd known her.

"You do that, Sarah." I smiled back at her. "I was always better at cussing anyway." I almost slapped the reins to go, but stopped and looked back at Aunt Sarah. My smile was gone now as I spoke in dead earnest to her. "On second thought, maybe you'd better pray for the heathens I'm going after, Sarah, 'cause when I'm done with 'em, they ain't gonna do nothing but shovel coal on the dark side of hell . . . and they'll think that's a pleasure, by God!"

"I'm sure they will, Ezra," I heard her say as I rode off. "I'm sure they will."

I rode hell-for-leather and then some, but I made it to that army camp I'd left just before sunset, leaving my mount at the livery with instructions on how I wanted him taken care of.

It wasn't hard spotting the general's quarters. The big chief's always got the biggest wickiup; I'd heard there were a lot of differences between the red man and the white man in wartime, but that remained the same in both societies. There was a sentry outside the entrance to the oversized tent and he only made one mistake when he saw me coming. He started bringing his musket to port arms, and about the time he had the weapon positioned, the barrel of Mister Henry landed up alongside his head and he collapsed like a toy soldier you've knocked sideways.

I threw back the flap and didn't have much need to get my eyes adjusted to the insides, for there were a couple of lamps already lit.

"See here, mister," the man behind the desk said. Bill Barnes was leaning against a corner of it. "You can't come in here like this!"

"Well, I just did, pilgrim, and I'm goddamn tired of being told what I can't do after I done it!"

"See here," he started again, getting blustery, "I'm General—"

"Name don't matter to me, mister," I said with a growl, "only that you got you some authority." Bill sat there taking it all in with a half smile. "I got me a sister lived in Lawrence, Kansas, is about the short of it, General. Seems some lads going by the moniker of Quantrill's Raiders took the town apart—"

"I know all about Lawrence and Quantrill, mister," he said, standing up and getting uppity. "Sergeant, remove this—"

Mister Henry lay in the crook of my arm, which was right in line with where the potbellied sergeant he'd spoken to stood.

"You move that rifle one inch, pard," I said, looking at the sergeant from the corner of my eye, "and all they'll put on your grave is a marker saying 'He died trying.'"

"Did you happen to know, *General*, that my sister got raped in Lawrence? Did you know that, too?"

"She what!" Bill said, more alarmed than I'd ever seen him.

"You heard it right the first time." If I said it cold and hard, it's because I felt that way.

"Believe me, Mister—"

"Hooker," Bill said, making the introduction, "Black Jack Hooker, General. He's the one I was telling you about."

"I'm deeply sorry about your sister, Mister Hooker. I have patrols out now searching for those men, Quantrill's Raiders."

"And you ain't caught 'em yet, have you?"

"No, sir, I've yet to receive any reports about—"

"Don't care 'bout your reports, General." Glancing at Bill I said, "It's a damn shame that a whole army can't come up with one single man out of four hundred who are supposed to be in this territory. You people would never last in the mountains.'' Then to the general I said, ''Gonna have to get 'em my own self, I reckon.''

I turned to go, then stopped at the tent flap, looking back at Barnes. ''By the way, Bill, they killed Jaime, too.''

I hadn't taken three steps outside of that tent before I had Bill Barnes walking beside me.

''Killed him in that barn next to Aunt Sarah's,'' I said, continuing to walk at a quick pace across camp. ''If he wasn't dead when they shot him, he burned to death in the fire.'' I stopped and gave Bill a hard look. ''Most of the town ain't nothing but ashes now.''

''Where are you going?'' he demanded. ''You think you can take on the whole world by yourself?''

We were at the edge of a fair-sized campfire when I stopped. I'd seen it when I rode in and had made a mental note to make it one of my stops while in the camp. The men, numbering a dozen or more, sat around the fire sharing stories. What had drawn me to them was the red stripe running down the leg of their trousers, as opposed to the yellow of a regular army soldier in the cavalry.

''Why not,'' I said, handing Bill Mister Henry, ''the world's taken on me, ain't it?'' From my shoulder I lifted the ammunition pouch I carried full of Mister Henry's .44s, handing it to him also. ''I wouldn't ask you to dirty your fists, William, so just watch my back if you will.''

He gave me a perplexed look as I walked into the light of the fire. The conversation stopped and they took me in while I slowly took off my beaver hat and tossed it aside. Right then it didn't make a difference that they were raiders for the North rather than the South. They were all worthless bastards, part of this war that had raped my sister. I'd come for business and they knew it.

''Jayhawkers, are you?''

''That's right,'' one of them replied with a mixture of pride and contempt. ''Jennison's Jayhawkers. What's it to you?''

''You're scum, the whole lot of you! Wolves that run in a pack just like Quantrill and his bunch!'' I said it loud, and you can bet they heard every word of it. Yes, sir. A handful of them got up, not liking my words.

"I've met scavengers I'd rather be with than you scoundrels. You go in after women and kids rather than face a man. Well, here I am, pilgrims! What're you gonna do to a *real* man?"

The half dozen that had risen were fair-sized men who now moved toward me, scowling.

"You got no cause to say that," one said in what sounded like a more peaceful tone than I'd expected. Over my shoulder I saw Bill holding one of his pistols in his hand. That must have been what was scaring these fellows.

"Oh, don't mind him, fellas, he's only watching my back. You can try to do anything you want to my front," I said.

That set them off and one of them took a roundhouse swing at my face. I ducked, sticking my right forearm up and over his as he followed through with the punch, my own arm locking on the crook in his elbow. It was unexpected and caught him off balance, as I brought the back of my fist down behind his ear, scraping it hard against his jawline, stunning him. In another quick motion, the flat of my foot kicked a leg out from under him, and I brought my right fist back into his face, sending him sprawling onto the edge of the fire.

"Ain't done that since I beat Big Pierre at Jackson's Hole," I said over my shoulder to Bill. I saw his face start to wince and ducked under another punch, bringing my fist into somebody's elsewheres as I came up under him. Fact is, my left hand found his throat as I grabbed hold of them personals, lifted him up over my head and threw him into the first Jayhawker I'd hit.

A third was making his way to me, either trying for a bear hug or to ram his head into my belly. I popped the flat of my hands on each of his ears, then grabbed those ears and pulled him upright enough to bring my forehead down across the bridge of his nose. Blood gushed forth as I threw him backward.

"Come on, you yellow bellies!" I yelled. I was expecting the whole crew to come at me at once, but not a one of them moved! I glanced over my shoulder, but Bill didn't even have his pistol out. "What's the matter, you afraid to fight?" Not even the three I'd just taken on made a move for me.

Then one of them snuck up behind me and split my skull open!

Chapter 14

When I came to, my head wasn't feeling any too good, at least not the portion that ran from the top to my eyeballs and front to back, which pretty much took in most of it. It was painful to open my eyes at first, then a mite easier once the voices in the background became clearer.

"Someone's holding a rendezvous inside my head and hasn't even asked me to it," I said as the focus came back to my eyes, and I saw a mischievous grin on Bill Barnes' face. A fancified back-east fellow I met once used the word pungent to describe the smell of manure and hay in a barn. Well, hoss, pungent ain't the word for it because it was downright nasty smelling in there. I could hear the horses milling around some and knew I was lying on a bed of hay not far from them. "Why is it I always wind up in a livery?" was my next question.

Bill smiled again. "You would've wound up in the stockade but I convinced the general you'd be a bad influence on the prisoners he's already got in there."

"General?" I squinted, then remembered what it was that had gotten me into this position in the first place. I worked myself up onto an elbow, rubbing the back of my topknot and the lump that was on one side of it. "Them Jayhawkers ain't too awful feisty, as I recall." I remembered taking on the three of them and then the campfire going out, taking all the light with it.

"If you take my advice, Black Jack, you won't go hunting them up again."

"Why? Just 'cause they know you by reputation and you ain't gonna be around next time?" I spit out, feeling the ire building back up in me from the night before.

Suddenly, the smile was gone from his face, and his tone was serious when he spoke. "Believe me, Hooker, it wasn't me that kept them from killing you last night."

"Do tell. Then what was it?"

"It was *him* with *that*," he said, throwing a thumb over his shoulder before stepping aside to give me a full view of Robert holding a sawed-off, double-barreled shotgun. "Whether it's fast or slow, no man looks forward to dying by a shotgun, Hooker. No man."

"How did you get here?" Slowly, I began to stand up, hoping I would be able to maintain my balance. "Got to be a first-rate tracker, did you?"

His right arm was still in a sling, although the bandage on his head was now removed, replaced by a hat. It was the look on his face that bothered me, for it hadn't changed since I'd last seen him, since I'd had that run-in with him in Lawrence. I'd seen that expression before, seen it on men who'd been touched with a bit of crazy in one form or another, and out here there were a lot of ways it could strike you. Losing your kin was one.

"As a matter of fact, Jaime gave me some lessons," he said.

"Look, fellas," Bill said on his way to the entrance, taking Mister Henry with him, "I've got some work to do, so I've got to be going."

"What've you got Mister Henry for?" The meanness was coming back to me, busted head or not.

"Oh, yeah, Hooker," he said with that mischievous smile again, "I was going to tell you—"

"Tell me what!"

"Tell you that it was me who whacked you on the back of the head last night."

He must have seen the rage in my eyes for he set the rifle down near the entrance and was gone in a flash. A half dozen quick steps and I had Mister Henry firmly in hand, but Bill Barnes was nowhere in sight.

"There's coffee out back," Robert said. "If it doesn't help your head, it should at least do something for your stomach."

As it was just past daybreak, his suggestion proved to be one of the better ones I'd heard so far that morning. Bacon and biscuits were the order of the day, and we ate in silence. It wasn't until I finished the last of my coffee that I asked him about the possibles sack he was carrying, which contained extra grub.

"Hunting killers, I figured we'd need enough food to track them down," was his reply, and I don't mind telling you that it fairly astonished me.

"Killers? *We?*" The food had helped dull the pain some, and maybe the knot on my scalp would look and feel less like pinewood by the end of the day. I shook my head back and forth, and winced. "No, son, I travel alone. Ain't partnered in years, not since the fur trade bottomed out."

"She may have been your sister, Black Jack, but she was my wife." Solemn was the only way to describe his tone, unless you throw in a bit of caution. I heard what he said, but not fully, not until I ran the words by one more time.

"Was?" My fist clenched into a ball, as hard as a rock.

"It was only an hour after you left, Black Jack. I guess she couldn't take it, couldn't stand any more. Somehow she found a knife and—"

"God damn it!" I yelled, not wanting to hear the tail end of that sentence any more than he wanted to speak it. I tore my hat off and threw it on the ground, not even caring about the pain in my head. It had been replaced by a rage I had never felt before, one I wouldn't wish on any man. "I'm tired of it!" I said just a tone lower. There weren't any mountains nearby to yell at, but I had to say it to someone, had to get it out.

"I spent thirty years carrying the memory of that boy with me, Robert, and that was painful. Now some bastard shoots me, I get hit over the head by a man who calls me friend, and I lose a sister to boot. Damn it, Robert, there's just so much pain a man oughtta have to take, and I've had enough!''

There was silence for a minute as we simply stood there, me trying to calm down, Robert watching.

''Then why don't we do something about it?'' he finally said, holding up his shotgun in one hand and tossing me Mister Henry with the other. I knew then I hadn't just spoken my own mind, but his, too. I kicked some dirt on the fire, putting it out, while Robert did a quick job of cleaning the coffee pot and skillet.

''We catch up with these yahoos, son,'' I said as we saddled up, ''and I'm gonna show 'em some tricks that not even the Blackfoot Indians have thought of yet!''

''We'll go through them like a flash of lightning through a gooseberry bush?'' He said it with a hint of a smile, likely remembering it from one of the stories I'd told Jaime.

I nodded my approval. ''Now you're talking, *pard*.''

The smile broadened as he heard that last word, and, knowing there wasn't any time left for palavering, we put the heels to our mounts.

It was late afternoon of the second day we had been gone from camp that he rode in. Like always, the mustang he rode was as independent as he was or he wouldn't have caught up with us that soon; and, like always, I knew who he was the minute I saw that big flop hat on the rise. Some things about Bill Barnes just wouldn't change, I thought.

The trail was cold, and to tell the truth I'm not sure either Robert or I thought we were following the right one. But, hell, son, you've got to do something, even if it's just waiting for trouble to happen. And when I saw Bill ride up, I knew we were headed for trouble. Of course, whether he knew it or not, he was in trouble, too.

''I didn't think it would take long to catch up with you two,'' he said, dismounting. That's when he found out about the trouble.

I hit him, as hard as I've ever hit any man. My fist

landed alongside his face, spinning him to the side so he careened off the flank of his horse.

"That hurt!" He was madder than a wet hen but didn't move from his horizontal position on the ground.

"I know," I said, giving him a devilish smile of my own. That was when he almost moved his hand toward one of his pistols but thought better of it.

"Tut tut, son." I shook my head in self-satisfied defiance. "You'd be dead before you got it out."

"Do you mind if I get up?" I was annoying him and he didn't like it.

"Nope." He gave me another killing look. "Normally, I don't approve of a man looking down on another when he's speaking his piece, but in your case I'm going to make an exception. Now, sonny, ever since I met you it seems you've been trying to one-up me. Well, that's going to stop right here and now, you understand, 'cause I've got more urgent things to take care of than tend to how great you feel 'bout yourself. Now, if you *comprende* that, you're welcome to pick out your share of the firewood and stay for a meal. Otherwise, you climb back on that hoss and get out of my territory. Soon as I finish my business, I'll be out of yours for damn sure. Which'll it be?"

He slowly got up, brushed himself off, and looked at the sweat-covered mount he'd just ridden in on.

"Think I'll stay for the food," he said, studying the horse. "Ain't neither one of us in much condition to go any further at the moment."

We went through about an hour's worth of silence, building the fire and making and eating the meal. It was at the end that Bill reached inside his jacket pocket and pulled out some papers.

"This is what I came to give you, Black Jack," he said, handing them to me. "You ain't the only one who's complained about the looting, pillaging and such that has nothing to do with the war. Just wanted you to know the general did something about it."

ORDER #11 was the title of it, and its purpose, if what I read was to be believed, was to do away with any number of guerrilla bands, including the Jayhawkers, assigning the men to the U.S. Army for regular duty in the war effort.

"Too many outfits like Jennison's are getting blamed for the work that's being done by common thieves, so the general put this order out as an official notice to disband them."

"Kind of late, isn't it?" Robert asked.

"I know how you feel, mister," Bill said. "I wouldn't enjoy losing kin either, but you've got to understand that Quantrill's is a Confederate outfit. I don't know who'll stop him or if he'll ever be stopped. Point is that the Union Army is doing its part to see another Lawrence doesn't happen."

"Well, now, William, I reckon from your side that sounds fine," I said, a frown coming to my face. "But you see, me and Robert never included ourselves in this damn fool war in the first place, so it don't make no never mind whether it was Rebs or Yanks that done in our kin. Robert here is finding out how strong on family us Hookers are, and you might say we just decided to declare war on whoever gets in our way until we find the scum that killed my sister."

Bill gave me a look from the corner of his eye.

"I thought you said she'd been raped?"

"When Black Jack left for your post that was all he knew, Mr. Barnes. She killed herself not an hour after he'd gone for help." The monotone of his voice, with just a touch of hatred to it, told me this was a dead man walking around before me—he just didn't know it yet. "So, you see, Mr. Barnes, that army order of yours is as useless as the paper it's written on. Your general may only want to disband the raiders, but Black Jack and I are going to put them out of business on a permanent basis."

"Far be it from me to stop you, friend," Bill said, holding up the palm of his hand to indicate no further desire to argue. "I've said my say. You do what you like. Most people do."

The sun wasn't quite setting as he rolled out his bedroll and prepared to turn in early. Then it hit me, something that had been bothering me about this man ever since I'd met him; something I'd always meant to ask him but was constantly interrupted before I could get to it. Now there were just the three of us and a long, lonely night ahead, so I figured I'd find out. He was getting ready to cover himself with a blanket and pull down that big flop hat of his over his eyes when I tossed a big chunk of deadwood on the fire and hefted the coffee pot.

"No, you ain't done talking tonight, mister," I said as the sparks flew from the newly fueled fire. Bill glanced at me, raising an eyebrow. I still held the coffee pot. "There's enough in here for a least a cup and a half more each."

"So?"

I squatted down on the far side of the fire and set the pot down to warm, all the while looking across those flames at the man I knew only as Bill Barnes.

"Mister," I said, with a bit more venom this time, "just who the hell are you, anyway?"

In slow, deliberate motion he pushed aside the blanket and hat, sighing like the kid who is caught with his hand in the cookie jar and has to fess up.

"What the hell." He took his empty cup and I poured us all some coffee. "Have a seat, boys, and let me tell you a story."

Chapter 15

It was like I'd suspected. His real name wasn't Bill Barnes, and when Sarah had called out for Jim in his presence that day in Lawrence . . . well, some habits are hard to break. Finding out that he wasn't just a freight driver and had done a few other "miscellaneous" jobs for the army, as he called them, explained his handiness with those pistols of his. As for his name, he thought sticking with Bill Barnes for the moment was a good idea.

I was also right about something else. Like I said, as soon as I saw him, I knew there was trouble ahead, for Bill had a mission and planned on using us to get it accomplished. Problem was we didn't find out about that until the next morning when we were saddling up.

"You'll be on your way back to camp then, Bill?" Robert asked. That's when he sprung it on us.

"Actually, I was thinking we might be able to help each other out." When he said that, I knew he already had in mind just what we were going to be doing.

"Do tell," I said, pulling the cinch strap tight on my riggings.

"Well, Black Jack, if what you said last night about recognizing that fella Jaime killed is true, I think I know where he and some of his partners may be." He gave us both a quick glance, looking for the kind of reaction he figured he'd get from us.

"If you know where they are, I'll follow you to hell and

back to get them," Robert said. There were times when we rode along that he was as quiet as could be, but bringing up the subject of the band of raiders who had done in his wife tended to bring the fire out in him. I knew he meant and would do exactly what he'd just said.

Me, I knew how young William worked, so I was a mite more curious than Robert.

"What's in it for you, lad?"

"I didn't know him all that long, Black Jack, but I kind of liked Jaime. He had the makings of a frontiersman, just like Johnny does." He wasn't feeding me a line now like he had before a time or two; the way he talked about those boys I knew he cared for both of them. He shrugged. "Maybe I just want to see a bit of justice done."

"What about the army? How do I know this ain't another one of those 'miscellaneous' jobs you're doing for 'em?"

"You can check with the general back at camp if you like and all you'll find is that I'm signed out for a leave of absence." That seemed to be all he thought he needed to say, for he mounted up and waited for Robert and me to do the same. I'd have to take him at his word; there was no use arguing the point, so I mounted up.

"Tell me something, Black Jack," Bill said when I was firmly in the saddle. "What's your stake in all this?"

It was a fair enough question.

"Well, William, I'll tell you," I said, levering a round into the chamber of Mister Henry and slowly lowering the hammer before looking at him. "You can keep your justice and all that. Me, I just want to see the faces of a few of those bastards before I kill 'em."

It was midday when we came on the town. But for being in the middle of Kansas it sounded like Old Taos at rendezvous time, with yelling and shouting and hoorahing in general. And that was from a half mile's distance. Robert was as confused as I was, which is when Bill started talking.

"One of the bad aftereffects of that Lawrence raid has

been that some towns, getting wind of it, have decided to evacuate. The news spreads like wildfire and they panic, and most often they leave with nothing more than what they've got on their backs. That's when the looters come in and pillage the town. Sounds like that's what might be taking place right now.''

Then a series of shots rang out and I cocked an ear to them.

"Sharps," I said, then paused. "Hawken," I said after the second shot and "flintlock," after the third. "Never did like them flintlocks.''

"Sounds like someone decided to give those fellows a fight for it," Robert said.

"Sometimes folks don't all make it out of the town before those yahoos descend on them," Bill volunteered.

I pulled back the hammer on Mister Henry.

"What say we make some of those roosters take flight?" I asked, looking at the men on either side of me. My answer came in both of them taking their weapons out and checking them. By God, it was going to be just like the good old days!

I'll tell you, hoss, my bones may be old and rickety and shot up and what not, but I felt an energy going through me now that most times I could only remember as a part of my youth. Maybe it's the memory of that youth that keeps us old bastards going like we do when these young pups need to be shown how. That and the hard-learned knowledge that fighting for your life is nothing to be taken lightly if you want to continue to tell stories about it. Me, I had a few more stories to tell.

Things must have been going right for us that day. The only man I could see taking a stand on the near side of town was a short, sawed-off blacksmith who had been firing these rifles I'd first heard. The rest of the yahoos were firing off pistols and riding or running through the streets as they did so, some shooting at the smithy, some wandering about drunker than hell. There were three bodies in the streets that I could see, although I couldn't tell if they were friend or foe. Fact is, these looters, if that's what they were, were paying so much attention to the return fire they were getting from the lone smithy that they didn't even notice us when we reined-in a scant thirty yards from the edge of town.

"I'd say this place needs a better clientele, lads. Let's clean some of the varmints out and bury the rest." I put heels to my mount, holding the reins in one hand, with Mister Henry pointing straight out in front of me like an extension of my arm. As soon as we were within range, Bill let loose with those pistols of his, leaving two horses riderless as we entered town and rode right into the big red barn the smithy was shooting from.

"And who might you be?" the stoutly built man asked with a more than casual cautionary air about him.

"Long as we ain't shooting at you, friend, I wouldn't be all that concerned," Bill said, dismounting.

" 'Sides, any man with that sort of collection of long guns is worth saving," I added, spotting at least half a dozen rifles in the corner. A variety is what this fellow had when it came to weaponry.

"Just how many and whom are we dealing with here, friend?" Bill said, taking charge as you might suspect.

"Might be some of that Quantrill gang," the smithy replied, loading another rifle as he spoke. "I heard they had split up into smaller groups and ridden off in different directions not long before these looters showed up. I think everyone's left town except four of us. I ain't leaving for nothing; worked too damn hard for this to want to start over again."

"Four?" I asked, curious as to the whereabouts of the others.

"The other three are right out there," he said, pointing to the bodies I'd seen earlier in the street.

"What do you think?" I asked Bill.

"Soon as they stop charging us, I'd say we ought to take after them."

"That shines, boy." I looked around and spotted Robert's horse, but not him. "Say, where'd that lad go?" My question was answered by a blast of a shotgun that could only have been Robert's. But the sound was nowhere close; it came from somewhere down the street. The man was out for revenge and had taken off without a second thought. Not that I could blame him, for if I'd been Robert and I'd heard what that blacksmith said about this maybe being part of Quantrill's gang, well, I'd have done the same thing. A man reaches a point, I reckon.

"Damn it!" I said.

"What's the matter?" Bill asked, reloading his own guns.

"Robert went off to see could he get hisself killed," I muttered, shoving a shell into Mister Henry's breech. "And I got an ugly feeling he's gonna get his wish, afore I can stop him. I'll be down the street, son. You give 'em hell," I added before running out of the livery entrance.

For about two seconds, everyone on that street must have thought I was the only one in town, for I swear there was more splintered wood flying than any beaver ever made chopping down a tree. Then I heard the alternating shots of the Colt's Navy .36 and the Army .44 Bill carried, booming as quick as you could count. I must have been about halfway to where I figured Robert to be, when I stopped to look over my shoulder and saw one rider leaning forward on his mount, blood streaming down the horse's neck, and another riding away with a grimace and a hand to his shoulder.

Another shot rang out and my hat went flying from my head—again! That tore it! Across the street I saw a man with a pistol in hand. He was laughing, likely at what he'd done to my hat. Mind you, there were splinters starting to kick up around me again, but I concentrated on this pilgrim. Face it, I wasn't in the funning mood. I took aim with Mister Henry and he was dead before he hit the boardwalks.

"Smart ass!"

A shotgun blast went off again and I knew for sure where I could find Robert, only thirty or so feet down the block. I ran as fast as I could and ducked into the store I'd heard the shot come from.

"Wait! Don't shoot! It's me!" I yelled all at once, as Robert twirled around toward me with his reloaded scatter-gun. You ever look down the business end of one of those things? Nasty, son, nasty. Makes you right squeamish, it does.

It was a general store we were in now, with most of the contents still intact except for the front window, which was nothing but jagged glass around the edges.

"Least you picked the right place," I said, looking at the corner of the store that was usually reserved for weaponry and its accessories. The cabinet held several shotguns and rifles, and the display case was filled with an array of pistols. If they weren't loaded now, you can bet it wouldn't be long before they were.

Behind me there was the sudden noise of boots landing hard on shattered glass. I was still halfway into turning, but Robert had taken a step to the right and pulled both triggers of his shotgun, sending the two hombres who had jumped through the full-length display window right back out into the streets. When they left, they were one helluva lot bloodier and deader than when they'd come in.

"You got sand, son," I said. "Now, get back to that rack and find something that's loaded, and *quick!*"

The urgency in my voice was anything but false, for the two who had just left us had a handful of friends across the street who were none too cheerful about their friends' death. In fact, there were over half a dozen of them charging right at me now! I shot two of them before they'd taken as many steps, and by the time they were out in the middle of the street, a third one had fallen. Another handful of horsemen made their way past them then, followed by heavy pistol fire that could have come only from Bill. I don't know if it was seeing all their support leaving them alone like that or it was the thought of dying that sobered them up and made them lose their courage real quick like, but whatever it was, they scattered like gophers at a rattlesnake convention.

A shot rang out behind me and I saw one of those pilgrims in the store with his finger on the trigger of his gun;

saw Robert jerk backward against a cash register of sorts. That yahoo was going to make sure he'd killed Robert, cocking his pistol a second time, but he never did do it, for Robert palmed that derringer of his and fired it twice into the man's heart. Then he sank to the floor.

I snapped off a round at a second ruffian coming through the back, but missed. I was on my way to the back entrance when I heard a pistol shot, and I went through that doorway ready for anything. I needn't have been, for the man lay dead in the alleyway, Bill Barnes' pistol smoke filling the air between the two.

"Hey, he's getting away!" came a yell from out front. "He's got my best horse!" I made my way to the front street and heard the blacksmith cussing something fierce as whoever was left of the band of looters rode out of town.

"Not for long, he ain't," I said, calm and determined. "Which one is he?" I asked as I took aim with Mister Henry.

"Second from the right, the bay."

No sooner had the smithy said the words than I squeezed the trigger and the man on the bay was soon a part of the dust being left behind by the riders. Without a word, the smithy ran after his horse. It was about then that I remembered I'd left Robert lying inside, wounded.

It was a chest wound and he was bleeding badly. He had to be in pain but instead he had a satisfied look on his face, the kind a man gets when he's done a job well, one he thought hard at the beginning.

"Gonna be all right, Robert, you hear," I said, kneeling down beside him and opening his coat. "I done plenty of doctoring in my day, didn't know that, did you?" I said it quickly to cover up the panic I was feeling inside, the loss I knew was coming.

"Don't give me that, Hooker," he said, coughing up some blood. "I'm dying and you know it.

"It was him," he added, slowly turning his head to look at the dead man beside him, the one he'd shot. "I saw him in Lawrence that day . . . fits the description Sarah gave me."

"You're just full of surprises, pard. Yeah, you got him good, you did."

Then he looked at me in a strange way, as if some revelation had come to him.

"Pard." A pained smile came to his face. "You mean that?"

I had told him it had been a long time since I had taken on a partner in anything, that I did better alone; then, finally, I had accepted his company, knowing his stake in the game. I never knew that being my partner meant that much to him, though.

"Why, sure, old hoss," I said, trying to find the right words. "You been my partner, Robert, all the way back to . . . why, all the way back to Independence when you and Callie got off the stage. You and me—"

I never did finish because with one last ounce of strength his hand gripped mine and he groaned—and he died.

"Brave man," I heard Bill say, and maybe that was all that needed to be said. Me, I was thinking of all the things Robert Carston and Callie had meant to each other, all the things they'd meant to me.

"Yeah," I said, slowly rising, "there's that, too."

There didn't seem like much else to do, now that the shooting was over, so I found a buckboard and got Robert out to what this town called a cemetery and buried him. Maybe someday someone would put up a proper marker for him, but I wasn't sure I had the time right then.

"Say, mister," the smithy, whose name was Ryan, said when I returned to town, "I sure do want to thank you for getting my horse back. Hell, for helping me out, you and your partner here," he added, nodding to Bill. "If there's ever anything I can do for you, you name it and it's yours, Mr.—"

"Hooker," I said, "Black Jack Hooker. Ryan, there's plenty I could have a smithy like you do for me, if you're as good as you say." I glanced at Bill, including him in the conversation. "Trouble is I ain't too awful sure we've got the time." Robert might have killed the one who had been responsible for Callie doing herself in, but now he was dead as well.

"You want 'em that bad?" Bill asked.

"In case you hadn't noticed, son, us Hookers is strong on family. Robert Carston might only have been my sister's husband for a short while, but by God he was family, and to me, William, that's all that matters."

"I'd give these horses a rest first, and ourselves, too, Black Jack. I recognized two of those yahoos leaving town and unless I miss my guess, I know right where I can find 'em." To Ryan he said, "You were right, they were part of Quantrill's gang." Turning back to me, he added, "They won't be hard to track down, Black Jack. Give these mounts a good feed and a day's worth of rest and we'll be talking to those fellas before you know it."

Ryan was a short but powerfully built man, sort of a sawed-off version of what you normally think of the village smithy as being like. Well, he wasn't a tall oak by any means, but judging from his build I'd say he came from the Petrified Forest at least. And if his work was as good as his brag, why, I had a challenge for him, something I'd been thinking on for some time now. You see, Mister Henry is outstanding when it comes to distance, and with as much use as he'd been getting of late, I'd become better at firing him than ever. Trouble was that if I got into another close-in shooting match—which seemed highly likely—I had a notion that I'd come in second best against the pistols that this crowd seemed to favor. Mind you, it wasn't a matter of being as good or as fast as Bill anymore, it was strictly a matter of survival. I was thinking Ryan might be able to help even the odds I knew we'd be facing.

"Anything at all, huh?" I said, giving him a devilish grin.

"Well, within reason."

"Ryan, how active is your imagination?"

"As a blacksmith? You just give me a try, Mr. Hooker." The grin hadn't left my face.

"Oh, I fully intend to, son. That I do."

Chapter 16

It was well past sunrise of the next day before he had it ready for me, but it was a beauty, that it was. When he handed Mister Henry back to me, the bottom part of the lever action had been redesigned just the way I'd told him I wanted it, enlarged to a circle a mite larger than my ham-sized fist. Fitted into the lever just below the trigger was a flattened piece of gray metal that would force the trigger back far enough to fire the weapon as the circular part of the lever closed on the stock of the rifle.

"What do you think?" Ryan asked with a good bit of pride.

"I do believe you've done it, son," I said, inspecting the new alteration to Mister Henry.

"What in hell is that?" Bill asked, sauntering over to see what we were up to.

"Our friend Ryan, here, has given us a bit more of an edge on those pilgrims you say we're gonna catch up with."

"How so?" he asked, still mystified by what he saw on the rifle.

I twirled the ring lever in my hand, the rifle and barrel going end over end. When they came back to their original position, the hammer was at full cock and ready to fire. Bill gave a low whistle of what I took to be approval if not admiration.

"Makes it a helluva lot easier to use when you're

mounted. Don't do too awful bad on the ground either, I'm thinking."

Bill raised a doubting eyebrow.

"Ryan, why don't you set up them whiskey bottles 'cross the street; do it any way you like," I said.

The man did as he was asked, spacing the bottles about two or three feet apart. When he'd returned, I planted Mister Henry's butt against my hip and fired the weapon three times. You didn't have to wait for the gun smoke to clear to know that I'd hit my mark on all three bottles, for the sound of their shattering was nearly as loud as that of the rifle itself being fired. The whole process couldn't have taken more than two seconds at most.

"Not bad, Hooker," Bill said, "not bad at all."

"You say we can catch up to these fellas right quick?"

Bill smiled mischievously. "Getting anxious to try Mister Henry out?"

"Now you've got the idea, son."

When we had saddled up, I asked Ryan to do me one last favor after we'd gone.

"Sure. Name it."

"Your cemetery's got a fresh dug grave in it, with shovels at the head of it. When folks hereabouts decide it's safe to come back to town, I'd appreciate it if you could have a headstone put up for him. Name's Robert Carston, C-A-R-S-T-O-N. Don't know when he was born or where, just put down yesterday's date for his death."

"Do you want an epitaph on it?"

I thought for a minute, then nodded.

"Yeah. Have it read: *He Was a Helluva Pard.* Ain't no one gonna know 'bout it but him and me, I reckon, but a man filling out a plot of ground oughtta have something written above him."

"Mr. Hooker?" Ryan said as I turned to go.

"Yeah."

"When the people in this town start coming back, they'll know about you two and your friend. I'll guarantee that."

"Obliged," was all I could think to say before we left.

* * *

It was nearing sunset when we came onto their camp, just like Bill had promised. Actually, it wasn't so much a camp as a broken-down building that resembled what might have once been a relay station for the Overland Company. It was located near a small wooded grove that had a spring, all of which made sense in a land with as much prairie as Kansas, with stretches of what seemed like endless miles of dryness and flat country. Several poles held the remains of the roof in place while the walls to the front and on either side were nonexistent, torn, or rotted away over the years. To the rear of the partial building was the grove of trees and the spring.

As in the raid on the Rebels that Bill and I had made in what seemed a decade ago, we rode up and dismounted on the far east side of camp. Drawing nearer, I began counting heads.

"Twelve?" I silently mouthed to Bill, who shook his head and held up the fingers of his hand twice, indicating he had counted ten. "Eyes must be getting bad," I mumbled and almost threw Bill into a panic, for as I spoke, a guard straightened up. I do believe it was the first time I had ever seen the man rattled.

"What's that?" the guard asked. "Who's out there?"

"Relax, Charlie," one of the other men said. "You're letting your nerves get to you. Boss'll be back tonight sometime. He's the only one you gotta look for."

"You think Quantrill's gonna try another one of those raids like we done on Lawrence?" another of the gang asked, leering. "They had some fine-looking ladies there, yes, they surely did."

When I heard the man say that, I was ready to kill him then and there and I would have if it weren't for Bill's strong hand on my shoulder, holding me still. It being my wounded shoulder made it a mite easier for him, I reckon. I gave him an angry look, but all I got back was a determined frown and a hard shake of his head.

"No," he whispered, "not tonight." Then he urged me to fall back with him into the shadows that now covered the land. I did, but you can bet it was grudgingly. When we were far enough away, we found a small gully and built an equally small fire.

"What did you stop me for!" I said, keeping my voice as low as possible while still letting him know I was mad. "You know as well as I do that those fellas are likely part of that Quantrill outfit!"

"I know," he said, "but it's that boss they mentioned coming back tonight. I've got a feeling I know who he is, and I've been after him for over a year now."

I was silent a moment and then it hit me. The blood started crawling up my neck and the rage built inside me like a roaring blaze. I reached across what little flame there was to the campfire and grabbed Bill by the shirtfront, pulling his surprised face over the fire so he could see mine.

"You said you were on leave!" I spit out at him. "No man on leave from the army goes out looking for trouble the way you've been doing! You *lied* to me again!"

"Ssshhh, quiet," he said, slowly undoing my fingers from the shirt. It surprised me that he hadn't drawn his pistols like he had during other confrontations with me. Maybe I'd finally caught him at something he couldn't deny and he figured there was no use in trying. After another moment's silence, he poured coffee in my cup, some in his own, and pushed his hat back on his head.

"The official record says that I've taken a leave of absence; you can check that if you like. But you're right, Hooker," he said, giving me a hard look over the fire that made me want to believe him just this once. "The general figured it might be better this way. You see, there've been a lot of information leaks in that camp, information that could only have been let out from inside. And I've got a feeling this so-called boss these men are waiting for is the one I'm trying to find." He shrugged noncommittally. "I didn't mean to get you involved, Hooker, but when it turned out we were both after the same group . . . well, you're a good fighter, especially with that Mister Henry."

"Why couldn't you have been honest with me? Why couldn't you have trusted me? Maybe I'm getting old, William, but after you've been out here as long as I have, you tend to expect that from a man who's been straight with you—or says he has."

"I know that, Black Jack. But you start to spying and all of a sudden you find that you can't trust anyone and have to lie about damn near everything you say. I wonder sometimes if I can even trust the general.

"Look, if you don't want any part of it, Black Jack, you ride on and I won't say anything about it. No one'll know."

That was about the closest I'd ever heard the man come to making an apology of sorts. Not that it meant anything to me.

"I'd know." I said it hard and even. "I spent thirty years carrying a bad memory that I never could justify to myself, son. I ain't about to do it again. Besides, yours may be army business, but mine's personal."

Coffee and hardtack was all we had that night, and the rest of the evening fire was spent in silence until we rolled out our blankets. Bill was laid out in his usual position, flat on his back, arms crossed, hands in easy reach of his Colts, his flop hat pulled forward over his face.

"Hooker?" he said from beneath the hat.

"Yeah."

"I really did like Jaime, you know. You might want to keep that in mind if you think you're the only one with a personal stake in this."

One thing about my sleep of late was that it sure had improved since Sarah had heard the truth about what had happened way back when. Maybe it's a clear conscience that did that for me; though out here it's mostly pure tired that'll close your eyes right quick at night. I slept straight through, only waking up when Bill nudged me.

Except it wasn't Bill!

He had a scruffy face and a hung-over look about him, but it was the business end of the shotgun he held that I noticed first. Like I said, they can be downright nasty.

"Crowell?" I heard Bill say, just coming awake. The man he was speaking to had a Union uniform on and looked an awful lot like the sergeant I'd threatened in that general's quarters. Seeing him full face I knew for sure it was the same man.

"They said you'd headed this way." I don't know if it was just the way the army teaches its sergeants to talk or if this fellow flat had a bad disposition, but there was a snarl to his voice.

"This the one you're looking for? Your traitor?" I asked Bill, slowly getting up, taking the situation in. There were two men with the sergeant, whom I thought I recognized from the raiders' camp. Yup, Crowell, or whatever his name was, was the traitor Bill had been looking for.

"Tie 'em up and bring 'em into camp," he told the two men. "We'll deal with them there." If ever there was a hateful glance thrown, it was the one sergeant Crowell gave Bill as he stomped out of the area, presumably back to the renegade camp.

"So that's your boss," Bill said to the man who was making a clumsy attempt at holding his pistol and tying him up at the same time.

"Ouch," I said, feeling the pain in my shoulder as I moved about. It was a genuine pain I felt, but it was the beginning of our getting out of this mess.

"Shut up, old man," the man holding the shotgun on me said, suddenly mean as all get-out.

"What did you say?" I looked at him from beneath my bushy eyebrows, moving slow and sickly like, the way young squirts like this one always figure us old geezers move.

"I said *shut up old man!*" he yelled, bringing the butt of his shotgun around and into my left side. I don't mind telling you that it hurt, too. I slowly straightened up, mumbling to myself and rubbing my side.

"That's what I thought you said," I replied, gasping for a mite of breath. Part of it was put on, but part of it wasn't, and I must have done a convincing job, for I even had Bill looking my way with a concerned face. I slowly turned my head left and right as though I had some trouble with the back of my neck.

"Too bad you youngsters ain't got no respect for your

elders, son." I worked my right hand up over my neck, and grimaced once or twice as I turned my head again. "Only one alternative to this life, you know."

"What's that, old man?" he prodded. It took everything I had to keep from tearing him apart then and there, but he had to know. He just had to know. I raised my head up some, making eye contact with him as my hand slid back just far enough.

"Death," I growled and pushed aside the shotgun with one hand while the other, holding my Tinker knife, slit the son of a bitch from one side of his neck to the other and blood began to spurt as he fell to the ground.

Bill's hands were almost tied, but he pushed the man before him back and it was just as that fellow turned toward me that I planted the Tinker in his heart.

"You ain't nothing but an old man," were his last words as he lay there in shock and dying. I yanked the knife out and it was the end of him.

"Smart ass!" I wiped the knife off on his shirt, then replaced it in its sheath in case it was needed again. After all, we weren't out of this fandango yet!

"Say what you like and any way you like it, William," I said, untying him, "but it all comes down to one thing." I glanced at the two dead men. "You breathe and you bleed."

"Won't get an argument from me on that," he replied, reclaiming his pistols and checking the loads. I did the same with Mister Henry, noticing about the same time as Bill did that the sun was about to come up.

"It's time," he said. I nodded.

We'd been lucky the guns hadn't gone off or the whole plan would have gone astray. As it was now, we were expected in camp—but tied up and fit to be killed. There were at least eight or nine renegades there now, maybe more if the sergeant had brought any help with him. Fact was, the odds were worse now than they had been that day so long ago when we went into the Blackfoot camp and made gone beaver of those Indians holding my brother. I had been scared to death that day, no denying it, but mad had got me through it, I reckon. Hell, being mad had gotten me through damn near every confrontation I'd had in life! Oh, I had Mister Henry with me now, but shooting at a moving target that shoots back is one hell of a lot different than firing at stationary bottles—*one hell of a lot different*! And you know something, hoss, I was scared to death again. I don't know about Bill; he looked about as cool as a cucumber, walking toward that camp. Truth was I'd never seen anyone quite like him under fire. He'd hold his own, Bill would. Me, well, friend, for a minute I took a notion in mind that maybe I was getting too old to be wandering around this frontier continually getting in trouble. Maybe it was time to settle down and make a living— if I got out of this scrape alive. Then I remembered Callie and Robert and Jaime and I realized that none of them had needed to die like they did. And I thought of Johnny who had a long life to live yet.

"Horse apples!" I mumbled under my breath. "This *is* a living." Bill gave me a strange look just before we parted, but all he saw was the mad in me getting madder.

Crowell must have felt confident that the men who were with him would be able to take care of us, for he had the rest of his gang around front, and no guards were posted. We could have ambushed them all, and I don't think Bill or I would have felt a twinge of guilt about it, considering what they'd done at Lawrence, but that wasn't the way out here if you followed a code. Bill was cold-blooded and he was a killer, no doubt about that, but I'd learned that the man preferred to face his enemy and settle any problems that way, rather than to back-shoot them.

We walked around the sides of that run-down shack about the same time and threw a surprise into those lads when they saw we were sporting our guns and minus the two guards. A couple of them began to go for their pistols but stopped short when I twirled Mister Henry and pointed him at them.

" 'Tain't healthy if you want to live long," I said. "Course, some of you ain't got long to live anyways."

"Why'd you give the Confederates information?" Bill demanded of Crowell.

"Money, you fool, why do you think!" Crowell shot back.

"That Rebel stuff ain't any good and you know it."

"I've got *gold*, Barnes," the sergeant said, every bit of greed in him showing in his eyes, "gold they stole from an army payroll."

"Which you gave them the information about."

"Of course! Look, Barnes, I'll split it with you, I'll cut you in—" He was talking faster than he normally would have; this man was scared, and it crossed my mind that maybe it was time to play an ace in the hole.

"Seems to me you're awful jittery 'bout dealing with him," I said to Crowell, nodding my head to Bill. Then, addressing the others, I said, "Seems like you might want to know what it is makes your sergeant here sweat so hard." They looked at one another, then at the sergeant, confused but knowing they'd been left out of some detail. "You said that Barnes name was an alias you were using, William? Wonder if these lads want to know who you were born as."

"Hickok is the name," he said, loud and clear, "J. B. Hickok if it matters." Putting them on edge was what I'd intended, and for the most part we achieved it as they all began exchanging wary glances.

James Butler Hickok was the name he'd been born under. He said he signed it as J. B. Hickok but used the Bill Barnes name for the spy work he was doing for the Union Army. It was when he had explained it all to Robert and me that night that I knew why he had answered to Sarah's "Jim." Some habits are hard to change.

"*Wild Bill* Hickok?" one of the younger, more impressionable men said in awe. A handful of them were beginning to look like they wanted no part of what was about to take place, and Crowell noticed it as well.

"Come on, people," Crowell rallied, "you ain't afraid of Hickok and this busted-up old man, are you? There's nine of us! We can take 'em!" Like I said, he was talking faster than you'd expect and making mistakes . . . like you'd expect. His biggest mistake was reaching for his pistol while he called me an *old man*. It was also his last mistake.

"Fill your hand, you son of a bitch!" I yelled, swinging Mister Henry around while he finished spouting off. I shot him high in the chest, and at that close of a range you can bet he flew backward a few feet before he fell to the ground dead.

That opened the ball, and pretty soon it seemed like me and Bill were the only ones standing our ground. I planted Mister Henry on my thigh, levered three rounds into him and fired in half as many seconds, sending three more of those pilgrims to hell—didn't matter to me how they got there, they could take a stubborn mule, for all I cared.

Bill had those Colts of his out and blazing before I even had my second round levered into Mister Henry. Lordy, the boy was fast! Two of the renegades were gut shot before you could flick an eyelash, and the other two had a real sudden change of mind about dying right then, and cut and run. Of course, by that time there was so much gunsmoke filling the air that Bill and I would soon be targets if we didn't move.

We did.

I thought I saw him run around the far side of the shack while I stepped over to the side I'd come in from. The horses were out back by the water, where two of the outlaws were doing their best to saddle up and get the hell out of there. I was standing out in the open now but really didn't care; I'd entered this game going up against a stacked deck and whittling down the odds some, but the game wasn't over yet.

One of them spotted me as he secured his saddle and began to mount. He must have been feeling gamey that day for he fired a snap shot at me that tugged at my sleeve. Again Mister Henry did the talking for me as I took aim and shot him out of the saddle.

But the surprise of my life came when Bill stepped out from behind the ruins of that shack and stood there, not twenty feet away, his pistols pointed at me! All that riding, I thought, all that shooting we'd done together, all of it was coming to an end now because he was as much of a killer as the rest. There was some blood on his shirt where he'd been hit but that inkling of a smile on his face told me he was enjoying himself. I knew he was going to kill me, knew I would never make it, but I said a silent prayer that my reflexes would carry through after his bullets pierced my heart, and swung Mister Henry's barrel toward him. Even as I began to move, he fired both pistols at once, and I found myself standing there in shock, for this wasn't what I'd expected death to be like! I didn't feel a thing!

"Smart ass," Bill said in that calm, even voice of his, but he wasn't talking to me. He was looking past me and when I turned I saw another of the outlaws lying dead on the ground. He had a pistol in hand and must have been the second of the two men who'd cut and run. I'd completely forgotten about him, and this lad calling himself Barnes or Hickok or whatever had saved my life.

"Now you're catching on, son," I said, looking back at him with a smile that said I was glad we were still a team of sorts.

Silence filled the air as I looked around at the gunsmoke slowly clearing the area, making visible the death and destruction that had been wrought here this day. Then I heard the gallop of a fleeing horse. Without a second thought I had Mister Henry up to my shoulder again, taking aim at the rider. I never made the shot, for Bill's hand forced the barrel of my rifle up into the air as a useless round left Mister Henry.

"What the—"

"Let him go, Black Jack," he said, looking first at me and then at the rider slapping his reins back and forth across his mount as fast as he could.

"But, he's one of—"

"You're never going to get *all* of 'em, Black Jack; it's just impossible. Good as you are, good as your rifle is, there just ain't enough ammunition or time to hunt 'em all down. There's better things in life to do.

"Letting that fella live may be the best thing you could
have done today, Black Jack. Let him spread the word
about what happened here today, about how Wild Bill
Hickok and a busted-up, old used-to-was mountain man
just shot the hell outta some raiders that thought they could
take the law into their own hands and get away with it."
Looking back at the rider who was all but out of sight, he
added, "Maybe some of these looters and raiders will think
twice before they try another Lawrence, Kansas, raid."

It made sense. If word of the Quantrill raid had spread
like wildfire, this minor massacre would inspire the same
sort of gossip. The story would grow way out of proportion
and soon it would sound like one of those big battles they
were fighting back east of the Mississippi. And if this young
lad named Hickok didn't already have a reputation, well,
he damn sure would once this story got around.

"Say, did you know you're bleeding a mite, son?" I
asked, pointing to what was most likely a flesh wound in
his arm.

"Speak for yourself," he replied, nodding his head toward my own arm, which I know noticed had a bit of a
sting to it.

The wounds were only scrapes, but bleeding tends to
make you powerful thirsty, so we all but drank that water
hole dry after patching each other up. Then we went back
to the area where we'd made our own camp and rolled up
our blankets.

"What about them?" Bill asked when he saw I was about
to saddle up.

"Leave 'em to the buzzards," I said, "they'd have done
the same for us." Bill shrugged and said nothing, which I
took to be a sign of his approval.

"Where you heading?" He mounted up.

I automatically turned the reins of my horse so he faced
west. "Lost everything I ever had in this part of the country, William. Reckon my stick floats there," I said, pointing straight in front of me. "Somewhere out there is the
Shinin' Mountains, and the closer I get to them the faster
I'll heal."

"Got some business just a bit west of here myself. Think you could stand being with me that much longer?"

I smiled. "Why not?"

And you know something, son, I do believe that last ride was about the only time that me and this youngster called Will Bill Hickok ever got to our destination without threatening to kill one another.

About the Author

Jim Miller began his writing career at the age of ten when his uncle presented him with his first Zane Grey novel. A direct descendant of Leif Erickson and Eric the Red, and a thirteen-year Army veteran, Mr. Miller boasts that stories of adventure flow naturally in his blood. His novels to date include SUNSETS, the six books in the Colt Revolver series: GONE TO TEXAS, COMANCHE TRAIL, WAR CLOUDS, RIDING SHOTGUN, ORPHANS PREFERRED and CAMPAIGNING, and Long Guns novels THE BIG FIFTY and MISTER HENRY.

When not busy writing about the future exploits of the Callahan brothers, Mr. Miller spends his time ensconced in his two-thousand-volume library filled mostly with history texts on the Old West. He lives in Aurora, Colorado, with his wife Joan and their two children.

JIM MILLER'S
SHARP-SHOOTIN' ST⊙RIES O' THE WAYS O' THE WEST!!

By the year 2000, 2 out of 3 Americans could be illiterate.

It's true.

Today, 75 million adults...about one American in three, can't read adequately. And by the year 2000, U.S. News & World Report envisions an America with a literacy rate of only 30%.

Before that America comes to be, you can stop it...by joining the fight against illiteracy today.

Call the Coalition for Literacy at toll-free **1-800-228-8813** and volunteer.

**Volunteer
Against Illiteracy.
The only degree you need
is a degree of caring.**

Ad Council Coalition for Literacy

LV-2